THE HOSANNA SHOUT

THE HOSANNA SHOUT

A Moroni Traveler Mystery

R o b e r t   I r v i n e

St. Martin's Press New York

Design by Judith A. Stagnitto

Library of Congress Cataloging-in-Publication Data

Irvine, R.R. (Robert R.)
    The Hosanna shout / Robert Irvine.
      p.   cm.
    "A Thomas Dunne book."
    ISBN 0-312-11418-4
    1. Traveler, Moroni (Fictitious character)—Fiction.
2. Private investigators—Utah—Salt Lake City—Fiction. 3. Fathers and sons—Utah—Salt Lake City—Fiction. 4. Mormons—Utah—Salt Lake City—Fiction.
5. Salt Lake City (Utah)—Fiction. I. Title.
PS3559.R65H67 1994
813'.54—dc20   94-21149
                                            CIP

First edition: October 1994

10 9 8 7 6 5 4 3 2 1

To Dominick Abel

ONE

A distant trumpet sounded. Atop the Mormon temple across the street, the Angel Moroni had his horn to his mouth as if summoning the dead.

Moroni Traveler opened his office window half expecting to receive the call. What he got was a faceful of smelter fallout from Kennecott Copper.

Behind him, his father said, "Mad Bill's at it again."

The bugle's note rose, becoming more aggressive. Bill had been practicing all week in the basement of the Chester Building, sounding what he called his Cavalry Charge.

"At least he plays better than Charlie," Traveler said.

"That won't stop them from getting arrested."

The pair of them, Bill, sometimes called Salt Lake City's Sandwich Prophet because of the hinged boards he wore advertising the tenets of his two-man church, and his lone disciple, Charlie Redwine, were marching in front of the temple gate. Halfway up the block on South Temple Street a uniformed policeman was already speaking into a handheld two-way radio.

1

The bugle changed hands.

"It's Charlie's turn," Traveler said, glancing at his father.

Martin remained seated at his desk with his back to the temple-facing windows. His feet were up, his hands laced behind his neck. "We haven't had an Indian summer like this in years, Mo. It must be eighty degrees." He drew a deep, sighing breath. "When I was growing up, October smelled like burning leaves, not Kennecott."

Charlie's first bugle note rose to a wail before trailing off as he ran out of breath.

"Indian summer should be quiet and peaceful," Martin added. "Like the church library."

"Is that where you were this morning?"

"I like to think of my dawn labors as a kind of penance."

Charlie tried again, this time hitting a note that made Traveler clench his teeth.

Martin said, "Not ten minutes ago, Charlie told me his ancestors confiscated Custer's bugle and have been playing it ever since."

"He's a Navajo, not a Sioux."

"He claims to be a Plains Indian at heart, a warrior of the old school."

Traveler had heard that before, Bill and Charlie going on about Indian warriors who gained honor by counting coup, by touching their enemies and getting away with it. Anybody could take a scalp from a dead man, Charlie contended, but it took real courage to approach your enemy intending only to play tag. Those who did so successfully were entitled to wear eagle feathers as a sign of their bravery, or so said Charlie.

Traveler saw no sign of plumage as he turned away from the window. "You heard them as well as I did yesterday, making up their own rules for counting Mormon coup. In this town, that could be dangerous."

"It was raining yesterday. They had to do something to kill time."

"You were the one who suggested the point system," Traveler said.

"I seem to remember that you thought it was a good idea at the time."

"We'd all been sampling Bill's sacramental wine."

"We should have guessed that Charlie had spiked it."

"Don't remind me," Traveler said. "I still haven't shaken the hangover."

"They probably feel as bad as we do, then."

"You weren't there this morning when Bill salted his coffee from Charlie's peyote pouch and said, 'As of today, we're changing tactics. Proselytizing by the laying on of hands. By counting coup in God's name.'"

Bill's proselytizing usually confined itself to panhandling, with Charlie rattling a carefully primed donation can in the faces of people passing in and out of the temple grounds.

Traveler groaned and turned back to the window in time to see Charlie standing directly in front of the gate blowing into the wrong end of the bugle as if something had become clogged inside. Beside him, Bill's hands banged rhythmically against his chest board as if he could still hear echoes of their Cavalry Charge.

"Do you remember the rules?" Traveler asked.

"Don't tell me they've actually started." Martin got up to look for himself.

Sunlight glinted off the bugle as Charlie held it to his lips.

"One point for deacons," Martin said. "Two for bishops."

"I was hoping I'd dreamed it."

"Members of the Council of Seventy count five, apostles ten."

"One hundred for the prophet himself," Traveler added.

"Forget it. They'd never get through his church security people, not alive."

Traveler caught sight of a police car at the head of Main Street, its red lights flashing, its siren silent as it edged its way through the midmorning traffic clotted around the bronze statue of Brigham Young.

"Women don't count," Martin said before returning to his desk. "No points at all. I don't think it has anything to do with their lack of status in the church. More likely Bill and Charlie are afraid of them."

As soon as the police car made it through the intersection, the officer holding the walkie-talkie stepped into the street and waved it to the curb a good hundred feet shy of Bill and Charlie.

"What the hell are they doing now?" Martin asked.

"Heading west." Traveler turned his back on the temple to sit on the deep granite windowsill. "In full retreat, sandwich boards flapping."

"I'd like to borrow a bugle and sound the retreat myself." Martin swiveled his chair to point at the Angel Moroni perched on his 210-foot spire, the highest of six that crowned the Mormon temple. "For the last three mornings I've been staring at a computer screen in the hall of records looking for our namesake."

"And?" Traveler prompted.

"Our luck with women continues. I don't know if they're smarter than we are or just more devious. Anyway, I give up. I can't find hide nor hair of a third Moroni Traveler."

With a grunt, Martin rose, went to the office door, opened it, and rapped a knuckle against the frosted glass where black, gold-edged lettering read MORONI TRAVELER & SON.

"I think Claire did it on purpose, got an old man's hopes up just to get even. She knew I wanted a grandson." His fingers traced the name Moroni. "Moroni Traveler and Sons. Is that too much to ask, for another generation of Travelers?"

No answer was expected; Traveler knew that.

"You should have married her," Martin said.

"You were the one who advised me against it," Traveler answered with a smile.

Nodding, Martin closed the door. "She was too much like your mother." He returned to his desk, this time settling into the client's chair.

Their one-room office on the third floor of the Chester Building held two side-by-side desks, each fronted by its own client chair. To avoid the pain in Martin's eyes, Traveler left the windowsill for his client chair and immediately had the feeling that they were both pretending to admire the temple view across the street.

Finally, Martin said, "I checked the records for both of Claire's towns, Milford and Milburn. I even tried Midvale. No luck. So much for that theory, that the letter M was the key. Claire's story must have been lies. For all we know she was never even pregnant."

"We have a witness who said she was."

"Sure. The same one we paid money to for information about M as in Milford."

Traveler was about to lay a hand on Martin's arm when his father stood up again and returned to his desk chair, leaning back hastily and closing his eyes. "They say everybody's listed in the church's computers. That's why I had such high hopes for Milburn."

When Martin opened his eyes, Traveler closed his. Claire was in the dark waiting for him, still sharp in memory, still alive, her reach long enough to play one last trick on him from the grave.

I've named the child Moroni after you.
He's not mine.
He has your name.
So does my father.
Maybe it's his.
Let me see the boy, then.
Only when you've paid.
What do you want?
That's for you to know.

Traveler rubbed his eyes until Claire disappeared. "It's time we gave up looking."

"Do you think she was lying, then?"

"Even if Moroni the Third exists, we have no claim on him."

"Blood ties, you mean." Martin pursed his lips. "Look at the pair of us. Blood isn't important."

"I thought it was when I was a boy."

"Your mother was foolish when she told you I wasn't your father."

"She never told me his name."

"Are you asking me for it again?" Martin said.

"Don't you think I should know?"

"Your mother wanted me to go back to using the name Moroni. Did I ever tell you that? She said it sounded more refined than Martin, more inspirational. You know what I told her? 'Kary,' I said, 'I had to fight my way through grade school to live that name down. I'm not about to change back to it.' "

A fresh Cavalry Charge—Bill's, judging by the sound of it—sent Traveler back to the open window. Their retreat had been a diversion only, the preparation for a new assault. Around the temple gate, people were scattering as Charlie approached doing a war dance and shaking his donation can like a tambourine. Directly behind him, Bill now wore a hand-lettered sign on his sandwich board. *God's touch is at hand. Feel it now before it's too late.*

"Christ," Traveler said, "I think they're actually going inside to count coup."

"It's that smelter smell. It's rotting everybody's brain." Martin joined him at the window, leaning out far enough to look west toward Kennecott. Traveler held on to him.

"It breaks my heart," Martin said, "to see what they're doing to the Oquirrh Mountains."

Traveler didn't bother to look. He knew what he'd see, Kennecott's vast mining and smelter complex chewing away at the Oquirrhs where they ran into the Great Salt Lake.

A shout went up across the street. Traveler pulled his father back inside. By then, there was no sign of Bill and Charlie, only a crowd surging around the gate. Up the block, the patrol car switched on its siren. Another, more distant siren answered.

"They're as good as in jail," Martin said.

Church security forces, looking very much like a SWAT team, seemed to materialize from nowhere.

"You stay out of it," Traveler told his father, but Martin

was already on his way out the door, forcing Traveler to run to catch up.

Down the hall, the elevator was waiting for them, the brass door open, its operator, Nephi Bates, crouched over the controls. "Ave Maria" spilled from the earphones hanging loosely around his neck. Beside him, Barney Chester, the building's owner, was waving frantically, urging haste.

"It's my fault," Barney said as soon as they were inside the grillwork cage. "I bet Bill and Charlie they didn't have the nerve to do it."

Nephi slammed the lever hard over. The elevator plummeted.

TWO

Uniformed police, reinforced by church security, had a path cleared to the temple gate by the time Traveler and Martin got there. Fire engines and police vans already barricaded South Temple Street, backing traffic to Brigham Young's statue in one direction, and all the way across West Temple Street in the other.

Yellow crime scene tape, stretching hand-to-hand between police officers, stopped Traveler twenty feet short of the gate. From behind the temple's granite wall, he heard Bill shout, "Feel the touch of God!" Judging by the volume, Bill had to be close by, since the walled temple grounds encompassed an entire city block.

"Sacrilege!" someone shouted in response, also from inside the walls.

Charlie answered with a war whoop that triggered rumbles from the crowd outside.

"What the hell kind of coup are they counting in there?" Martin said.

Before Traveler could answer, a door slid open on one of the vans. Two sharpshooters, both armed with military assault rifles, jumped out. At the same time, firemen unhooked a ladder from a nearby truck and carried it forward, flanked by the riflemen. When the crowd parted to let the group pass, Traveler moved to intercept Lieutenant Anson Horne who was bringing up the rear.

"Christ," Martin said into Traveler's ear. "It would be him."

With Horne was his partner, Sergeant Earl Belnap.

"Go back to the Chester Building and call Willis," Traveler told his father. "We're going to need some help."

Most times Martin might have argued, since he considered Willis Tanner more trouble than he was worth when it came to favors asked. But this time, he merely nodded and trotted back across South Temple Street.

Traveler caught Horne's attention.

"What the hell do you want?" the lieutenant said.

"That's Bill inside."

"I should have known. The call said some kind of terrorist had stormed the temple grounds."

"Two terrorists," Belnap added, running a hand over the short nap of his military haircut. He had the forearms and shoulders of a serious weight lifter.

"Charlie's with him," Traveler confirmed.

Horne tapped Traveler on the chest. "Just stay out of my way."

"I've called Willis Tanner for help," Traveler said.

"I heard he was on his honeymoon."

Traveler shrugged, knowing that Willis's name could work miracles when whispered in the right ears. Tanner, Traveler's friend since childhood, was in charge of public relations for the church and a spokesman for the prophet, Elton Woolley.

"I suppose you want to go inside," Horne said.

"Bill trusts me."

Horne took a deep breath and nodded at his sergeant. "Bring him along. It's easier than arguing."

Traveler forced himself not to struggle against Belnap's

painful grip. The sergeant took Traveler's acquiescence as a sign of weakness and elbowed a kidney, no doubt a technique he'd learned during his stint with the LAPD. Traveler was about to unclench his teeth and protest when they cleared the gate and caught sight of Bill. Even Belnap must have been stunned by the spectacle, because his grip went as slack as his mouth.

Bill was perched atop the Sea Gull Monument, clinging to the bronze birds that commemorated the thousands of gulls who'd devoured the locust plague threatening the harvest of the first Mormon pioneers.

Horne stopped in his tracks. "It *is* sacrilege."

"What do you expect from a Gentile," Belnap answered. Since moving to Salt Lake, Belnap had transferred the LAPD's hard-nosed attitude against blacks to non-Mormons, or Gentiles as they were called in Utah. He was the perfect partner for Horne, a second-generation cop and third-generation Mormon bishop.

Church security, augmented by the regular police and the sharpshooters, surrounded the sixteen-foot Doric column at a distance of about twenty yards.

Bill raised one hand toward heaven. The gesture cost him his balance and he had to grab a bronze wing to keep from falling.

"Shoot him off of there," Belnap said.

The sharpshooters, apparently seeing that Bill was unarmed and in no position to harm anyone, were concentrating on Charlie, who still had the bugle.

"Sound the call," Bill shouted.

From the lip of the monument's granite reflection pool, Charlie raised the bugle to his lips and produced a shrill, ragged note.

Horne waved the sharpshooters back, then signaled two of his regular officers to move in and secure the Indian. Once Charlie was handcuffed, the church security men, all dressed in suits and ties like the ex-FBI agents they were, faded back to the visitor information building near the gate. There was no sign of the armed church SWAT team that Traveler had seen from his office window.

"I still say we shoot him," Belnap said.

"Does anybody know what the hell he's doing up there?" Horne asked.

Movement in the doorway of the Assembly Hall beyond the Sea Gull Monument caught Traveler's eye. The man who stepped out of the shadows into sunlight was tall, white-haired, fragile-looking, and somewhere in his seventies. His suit was black, his shirt starched and white, his tie gray; his appearance made Horne catch his breath.

"Moroni," Bill called from his perch, "it wasn't my idea to climb up here. They chased me."

"That's Josiah Ellsworth," Horne murmured under his breath. "The apostle."

Ellsworth was coming directly at them across the lawn, ignoring the winding paths. Church security reappeared, four of them materializing from the trees and shrubbery, better dressed than most but still armed with that hard-eyed FBI stare. They closed around Ellsworth, keeping a respectful distance but near enough to provide protection.

"I didn't see them waiting for me," Bill said. "I didn't have a chance."

Traveler looked for signs of additional security inside the ten acres that made up Temple Square. The Tabernacle was big enough to hide an army of them, as was the Assembly Hall and Museum. Joseph Smith's life-size bronze statue provided cover too, not to mention the Temple Annex, an ivory-painted Moorish building made of oolitic limestone.

Josiah Ellsworth stopped in front of Lieutenant Horne and said, "Do you recognize me?"

"Yes, sir."

Seen up close, the apostle had a young face, unlined and untroubled. He was Traveler's height, six-three at least.

"That man tried to attack me." With a tilt of his head Ellsworth indicated Bill. "The Lamanite is his accomplice."

11

According to *The Book of Mormon,* Indians were thought to be descendants of one of the lost tribes of Israel, known as Lamanites.

Ellsworth turned his gaze on Traveler, who sensed recognition in the man's eyes.

"Are you with the blasphemers?" he asked.

"I'm a friend."

Nodding, Ellsworth said, " 'And it shall come to pass that there shall be a great work in the land, even among the Gentiles, for their folly and their abominations shall be made manifest in the eyes of all people.' " When he finished speaking, the apostle looked expectantly at Horne.

Horne wet his lips; his Adam's apple shimmied. A twinkle in Ellsworth's eyes said he was used to provoking such a reaction.

Traveler got Horne off the hook by saying, "Are you hurt, Mr. Ellsworth?"

"Thank you for asking, Brother Traveler. He touched me on the shoulder, nothing more. What else he had in mind I don't know. My friends here"—a brusque gesture indicated the security men—"didn't give him the chance to go further."

"That's fifty points," Bill called down to them.

Traveler didn't look up and didn't respond.

"Counting coup," Bill clarified.

Apostles counted ten points, Traveler recalled. The prophet one hundred. He didn't remember any mention of fifty-point scores.

"An eagle feather earned," Charlie said. His words got him hustled back to the tourist center where the firemen were waiting.

Under different circumstances, the situation might have been funny, but in Salt Lake, assault on a church dignitary, even if no more than a touch, could earn prison time.

"I apologize for my friends," Traveler said. "I know it was inexcusable, but it was a game, a bet, nothing more."

"I have studied Lamanite culture," Ellsworth said. "I am familiar with coup counting. But it can be earned only if those you touch are your enemies." He turned to look up at Bill.

" 'Wherefore, let no man glory in man, but rather let him glory in God, who shall subdue all enemies under his feet.' "

With that, the apostle smiled and headed toward the temple.

When he was out of earshot, Horne turned to Belnap. "Get a ladder in here, for Christ's sake. Let's get that bastard down before we lose our jobs."

Coming from a man like Horne, profanity was unusual; hearing it uttered on the temple grounds made Traveler fear for Bill's safety more than ever.

"Let me get him down," Traveler said. "If I do it, there won't be any trouble."

"There won't be any trouble my way either."

Two firemen, escorted by Belnap, arrived carrying a light-weight extension ladder; they hesitated at the reflecting pool, staring up at Bill as if contemplating his potential for violence.

"He could take someone with him," one of the firemen said.

"It can't be more than a fifteen-foot drop," Horne said.

"Then we'll hold the ladder while *you* climb up there."

"Leave it to a Gentile," Traveler said. "Back off a ways so Bill won't panic."

The firemen looked to Horne for guidance.

The lieutenant pointed at the monument. "You heard me. Set up that ladder."

They exchanged shrugs before wading through the ankle-deep water to lean the ladder against the marble column. The top rung was two feet shy of Bill, whose arms and legs were wrapped tightly about the pillar. As the firemen were about to extend the ladder, Horne said, "On second thought, I don't want you scratching the marble."

"You're damn right," Belnap said. "Shoot him off of there and be done with it."

Traveler was wondering if it was time to evoke Willis Tanner's name again when Horne pointed a finger at him. "We'll send Moroni up there after all. If something goes wrong, we can kill two birds instead of one."

Without a word, Traveler waded in. The water smelled of chlorine and felt icy despite the warmth of Indian summer.

———•———

"Consider yourself baptized," Bill called down to him.

Water from the hem of Bill's robe dripped on Traveler's head as he adjusted the ladder until it stopped wobbling. That done, he climbed far enough so he wouldn't have to raise his voice.

"I know what you think," Bill said, "but counting coup is no game. If only one of those I touch sees the light, then I have done God's work."

"It's me you're talking to."

Bill laid his head against the marble globe on which the bronze gulls were landing. "I struggle in the wilderness, Moroni. I walk the streets. I proselytize. And still I have only Charlie to show for my efforts."

"Prophets are seldom appreciated in their own time."

"Don't I know it. Donations are off. Charlie and I can barely make ends meet."

"You have a roof over your heads."

"The basement of the Chester Building is not a proper place for a prophet."

"Maybe I can talk Barney into lending you a vacant office."

"I need a sanctuary, Mo, a place in which to pray." Bill raised his head to stare up at the temple towering two hundred feet above them. "I envy them, you know. Their faith, their diligence. Think of the love that went into building such a monument."

Bill let go with one arm, nearly losing his balance, to gesture at the temple. "What kind of people were they, Moroni, those pioneers who crossed the Great Plains and the Rocky Mountains to claim this desert sinkhole and call it their promised land? They arrive too late to grow a crop; they have meager provisions. There is no guarantee they will even survive the first winter. Yet what do they do? Do they despair? Do they curse their luck?"

Bill shook his head. "I'll tell you what they did. They gathered around Brigham Young, their prophet; together they walked this very ground. And there . . ." Bill pointed at the temple once again. "There Brigham thrust his cane into the earth and said, 'Here we will build the temple of our God.' "

Bill began to tremble. Traveler eased up another rung to catch him if need be.

"I stand in awe, Moroni. They marked the spot and bided their time, building their homes and planting their crops, until finally six years later the temple's cornerstone was laid. For the next forty years they worked on God's house. They cut the great granite stones from the Wasatch Mountains twenty-six miles away, each stone so heavy it had to be hauled by four oxen, a trip that took four days. Forty years to the day after the temple was begun, the capstone was laid and fifty thousand people gathered here to give the Hosanna Shout."

Slowly, Bill raised one arm and then the other. Traveler lunged, wobbling the ladder, to wrap his arms around Bill's legs. Out of the corner of his eye, Traveler saw more firemen arrive carrying stretchers.

"Listen to it, Moroni. 'Hosanna! Hosanna! Hosanna! To God and the Lamb! Amen! Amen! Amen!' "

"Grab hold, you're slipping."

"Have faith," Bill said. "Those who were here that day said the ground trembled with the raising of their voices. Will the ground tremble for me one day?"

"If you don't hold on, it will."

"I'm not afraid of becoming a martyr."

"I am."

"You're named for an angel, Moroni. You have nothing to fear."

"What about Charlie?"

"My apostle would be lost without me, I admit that. I will descend for his sake."

"I'll go down first and hold the ladder," Traveler said.

As soon as his feet were in the pool, Traveler looked up to see Bill's tennis shoe feeling around for the top rung.

"Left a little," Traveler said.

"My legs have gone to sleep."

"Don't move, then. I'll come back up."

"Look out!"

As Bill let go, Traveler shoved the ladder out of the way and tried to break the fall. He succeeded except for one outthrust leg that hit the lip of the pool. Bone snapped. Bill screamed as he and Traveler landed on their backs in the cold water.

They were immediately surrounded by police. Horne himself helped load Bill onto a waiting stretcher. As the attendants started to lift it, Bill grabbed hold of Traveler's sleeve. "I didn't realize who he was, Moroni. Not at first."

"Who?"

Bill tugged until Traveler crouched down beside the stretcher.

"Ellsworth is more than an apostle," Bill whispered. "He's the White Prophet."

"Don't start, Bill, not now."

"He exists, Moroni. I knew that the moment I touched him."

Traveler settled back on his haunches and stared at Bill. Recognition by touch was probably one of Bill's euphemisms. Most likely Josiah Ellsworth was known to Bill before, by sight and reputation at least. Whether or not he was the White Prophet was another matter.

"He doesn't exist," Traveler said. "He's legend."

"You resemble him, Moroni. For a moment, when I first saw him, I thought he was you." Bill sighed deeply. "What will they do to me for touching him?"

Traveler had heard stories about the White Prophet since childhood. The Catholics had their Black Pope, or so the litany went, and the Mormons had their White Prophet. In the case of Catholicism, the Superior General of the Jesuits was actually called the Black Pope because of his black cassock. In the case of the White Prophet, the color had been chosen—the opposite of black—because all things Catholic smacked of the devil. Yet there was something devilish about the White Prophet too. His name, like the bogeyman, was often evoked to scare unruly children. *The White Prophet will get you and carry you off to burn in hell.* His mother's words, echoing years later.

According to tradition, the White Prophet was the leader of the Danites, sometimes called the Brothers of Gideon or the Sons of Dan; he was a shadow prophet picked from among the apostles, the leader of the avenging angels sworn to destroy the enemies of the Mormon church.

Horne tapped Traveler on the shoulder. "We'd better take him to the hospital."

As the stretcher was raised Bill turned his head toward Traveler and mouthed, "Pray for me."

"Is he under arrest?" Traveler asked Horne.

"What do you think?"

"I'll post bail," Traveler called after the departing stretcher, which was accompanied closely by Sergeant Belnap.

"Sacrilege should be like murder," Horne said. "No bail."

"Am I free to go?"

The policeman waved Traveler toward the gate. Walking away, Traveler felt as if his back were a target. He almost missed seeing his father, who was waiting beside Charlie at the tourist center. The Indian raised his hands, displaying the handcuffs as if they were a prize for counting coup.

"I think you ought to ride in the ambulance with Bill," Traveler said to the Indian. "He thinks the Danites are after him."

Charlie nodded. "The White Prophet is a formidable enemy."

"Not you too?"

"Charlie's under arrest," Martin said. "He's not going anywhere but jail."

"I need medical attention," Charlie said and collapsed, pretending to faint.

"He should have been an actor," Martin said as the Indian was carried away on a second stretcher. "Maybe we'd better go along just the same."

"Don't tell me you believe in the White Prophet?"

"In the land of Zion it's always best to be prepared."

"Did you reach Willis Tanner?"

"I left a message," Martin said.

Church security was waiting for them at the gate, two men looking every bit the equal of Apostle Ellsworth's personal bodyguards.

"If you'll come with us," one of them said, displaying a compact briefcase, "we have a phone call for Moroni Traveler and Son."

Traveler and Martin followed the pair into the museum, adjacent to the tourist center, where the briefcase was set on top of a glass display case filled with Mormon gold coins. A card key opened the briefcase and activated a cellular phone, fitted with an electronic scrambler, which was handed to Traveler. After that, the security men moved to a discreet distance.

"Mo," Willis Tanner said, his voice clear and free of static, "I got your message. I suppose it's about Mad Bill and that Indian. Assault is a serious offense. So is trespassing."

Traveler angled the phone so Martin could hear.

"What's the charge going to be?" Traveler said.

"Josiah Ellsworth is an important man."

"How important?"

"Don't believe everything you hear, Moroni."

"I thought you were supposed to be on your honeymoon."

"At this moment Lael and I are passing through Spanish Fork on our way to Manti. It was the prophet's idea really, honeymooning in our state's temple towns. Manti's first, then St. George. After that, our schedule's open. Maybe we'll double back to Provo, maybe not. I'm sorry you couldn't be at the wedding, Mo. Had you seen the light you would have been my first choice for best man."

"The price was too high," Martin shouted at the phone, referring to the ban against Gentiles setting foot inside the temple.

"We'll never let up, you know," Tanner said, "not until we have both our Moronis back."

Martin snorted. "Get to the point, Willis. Did you call to help Bill, or not?"

Tanner chuckled. "Lael and I thought it would be nice to

turn the tables on you two. We want to give our Moronis a wedding present."

Martin shook his head. "I don't like the sound of that."

"I owe you one. Mo knows that."

"I don't recall a debt," Traveler said.

"Lael saw you first, Mo. You stepped aside."

"You know my luck with women."

"Lael says she's going to play matchmaker one day."

Martin groaned. "Don't ask for a favor in return."

"Did you hear me ask for anything?"

"You always do," Traveler said.

"Have faith, Moroni. 'Behold I will lift up my hand to the Gentiles, and set up my standard to the people; and they shall bring thy son in their arms, and thy daughters shall be carried upon their shoulders.' "

"I don't trust him when he starts quoting scripture," Martin said.

"You will," Tanner said. "I have a lead on the child, on Moroni Traveler the Third."

"Don't start that," Martin said. "We're not even certain he exists."

"What kind of lead?" Traveler asked.

"How old would he be now?" Tanner answered. "Two, going on three?"

"That's right."

"The army of the Lord is growing," Tanner said. "Eight million Mormon saints and counting, more than enough to find one small, lost soul. And you know the prophet. He keeps an eye on his Moronis. 'If one is lost,' he told me, 'send forth the Legions of Nauvoo.' "

That was Tanner's way of reminding Traveler of the church's power. Not only was it the richest in the country, but the fastest growing. As for the Legions of Nauvoo, the first one was raised in Illinois by Joseph Smith, who rode at its head on a horse named Charlie, determined to defend the faith. But in the end, the legion was unable to keep him from being murdered and his people driven from Illinois.

"When you consider the missionaries we have all over the world researching ancestors," Tanner went on, "we're the real detectives, not Moroni Traveler and Son."

"If we're ever going to add another *and son,*" Martin said, "get on with it."

"We have a man in Park City, Giles Wilmot. He's semi-retired, a part-time doctor and part-time church historian who's uncovered a Moroni Traveler that hadn't shown up before on our genealogy computers."

Traveler said, "Are you telling us he's actually found the boy?"

"You must have faith," Tanner said.

"I know you, Willis. There's more to this than you're telling us."

"Easy, Mo," Martin said. "Maybe I've misjudged him. Maybe he's the answer to an old man's prayers for a grandson."

"As I said before," Tanner said, "it's my gift to old friends. Just don't ask me to help with the Chester Building."

"What the hell does that mean?" Traveler said.

Tanner hung up without answering.

THREE

As soon as they cleared the temple gate, Traveler and Martin paused on the sidewalk to stare at the Chester Building across the street. The last of the police cars was just pulling away from the curb. Visitors were again lining up for tours of the temple grounds. Traffic was back to normal for a Wednesday morning. The warm October air smelled of sycamore and Kennecott.

Traveler said, "Willis was with us when Bill and Charlie first started talking about counting coup."

"I saw the three of them huddling together yesterday in the lobby."

"Why would he do that on the eve of his honeymoon?"

Martin shook his head. "Willis always had the knack of getting you into trouble while escaping the consequences for himself."

"That was a long time ago."

"People don't change."

"These days Willis doesn't make a move without approval from the prophet."

"That's what worries me," Martin said.

"We're both sounding crazy. Willis wouldn't encourage Bill to count coup against someone like the White Prophet."

"Your mother used to threaten us both with the White Prophet, if you remember. Usually she'd been nipping at her homemade elderberry wine, which she considered exempt from the Word of Wisdom."

"Kary was a great believer when it suited her."

"She claimed to know the White Prophet personally," Martin said. "Your mother had more friends than anyone I ever knew. Of course, she changed them once a month."

"Did you ever meet Ellsworth?"

"Through your mother, you mean?" Martin shrugged. "That was a long time ago. You were a baby."

"I've never heard that Ellsworth was special among the apostles. He looked harmless enough to me."

"You saw him?"

"We talked for a moment. I did my best to persuade him that Bill didn't mean any harm."

"And?"

"He looked me in the eye and spouted scripture."

Martin sighed. " 'Fear not, little children, for you are mine, and I have overcome the world, and you are of them that my Father hath given me.' You see. There's enough in the good book for everyone."

Traveler wondered if he was missing something. Had Martin finally decided to give him a clue to his biological father?

You are a child of the prophet came back to him. His mother's words spoken often enough. Had she meant it literally?

"Are you trying to tell me something about my father?" Traveler asked.

"I raised you. What else is there to know?"

Your father is an important man, Kary had said. *A man with a future. Not a private detective with an office in the Chester Building, but one of God's anointed. The blood of the apostles runs through your veins.*

"I was remembering what Kary used to say," Traveler said. "Ellsworth is my height."

"Women do that, mothers in particular. They plant things in our heads that keep on growing and sprouting for the rest of our lives."

"Then we'd better find out who's raising Moroni Traveler the Third."

"He's waited two years. He can wait until we check on Bill and Charlie."

"Don't forget Willis's remark about the Chester Building." Traveler pointed across the street to where Barney Chester was waving frantically at them.

As soon as they reached him, Chester removed the usual unlit cigar from between his teeth, made a show of looking both ways up and down the sidewalk, and said, "The church is after me."

Gone was the tough-guy sneer he'd been cultivating ever since someone said he looked like Edward G. Robinson. "They're going to take away my namesake."

"Good old Willis," Martin said.

"They're inside right now," Chester said.

Martin sighed. "I've heard enough about church conspiracies, Danites, and the White Prophet already this morning."

Chester grabbed Martin's arm. "I'll show you if you don't believe me."

He led the way through the bronze revolving door, across the lobby's marble floor, to where his cigar stand was sandwiched between two massive Doric columns. There, a man in a gray, well-worn suit was bent over the glass-topped display case, shaking his head as if he couldn't believe the Chiclets, Sen-Sen, and bags of Bull Durham inside.

Without looking up he said, "You told me you were coming right back." He blew on the eternal flame, causing it to flicker momentarily. The flame, according to Chester, was a pilot light for those who enjoyed the religious fulfillment of cigar smoking.

"This is Emmett Yancey," Chester said. "He's an appraiser for the city."

Yancey, a slender, balding man clutching a clipboard that contained a sheaf of papers an inch thick, turned to peer over the top of his glasses at Traveler. "I don't care how big you are. Intimidation won't work. If I don't do the job, someone else will."

Traveler backed off a step.

"Hold it," Martin said. "We don't even know what's going on."

"They're stealing my building," Chester said.

Yancey adjusted his glasses. "I told you before. I'm here to make certain that you receive fair compensation."

"Who wants the building?" Traveler said. "The church or the city?"

"The church," Chester said.

"I work for the city," Yancey said. "The church can't exercise eminent domain."

"I've got it on good authority," Chester said.

Yancey waved his clipboard. "I've shown you the paperwork. Now, are you going to accompany me or not?"

Chester sagged, shoulders, chin, and stomach; even his cigar drooped from between his teeth.

"You'd better do what he says," Martin said.

Immediately, Yancey headed for the revolving door, stopping just short of it. "Look at that damned thing. It's brass, it's heavy, it's out of date and probably not even worth salvaging." He pushed the door experimentally, consulted his clipboard, and made a checkmark with his pencil. "People can get stuck in these things, you know, maybe even break an arm or a leg. It's a lawsuit waiting to happen. This whole place is, if you ask me."

"My building is genuine art deco," Chester said.

Shaking his head, Yancey toured the lobby. "Look at those gilt cornices and that grillwork over the heating vents. They haven't made that kind of thing for years. Maybe if we're lucky, it can be melted down for scrap. If not, we'll have to deduct it from the price."

"Those are collector's items," Martin said.

"You're welcome to make a bid on them," Yancey said. "As for your marble floors, Mr. Chester, they're not only a hazard when wet, but far less practical than industrial carpet."

"Dammit. That's Italian Carrara."

"A lot of people think they can stick the city and get rich. That's why I'm here. I'm paid to protect the taxpayers' money."

Traveler said, "Mr. Chester has rights too."

"He can always resort to the courts. If you ask me, though, we'll be doing him a favor by taking this place off his hands and bulldozing it."

Chester ground his cigar into an ornate, standing brass ashtray. "They served me papers first thing this morning, Mo. I hadn't heard a peep before that. The church wants to build a parking lot for the temple. Nephi Bates told me so not ten minutes ago."

Martin squinted at the appraiser. "Is that right, Mr. Yancey?"

"I work for the city. They tell me what to do, I do it."

"What do they want the land for?"

"You'd have to ask the powers that be."

"In this state, that's the church."

Yancey shrugged and headed for the men's room.

"We'll wait for you out here," Traveler said.

"You're welcome to come if you want. It's part of the inspection."

When the door closed behind him, Traveler turned to Chester. "You've been saying for years that Nephi Bates was nothing but a church spy, so why are you listening to what he has to say now?"

"He makes sense, Mo. The city builds a parking structure and then leases it back to the church. That's what Nephi thinks, anyway."

"How would he know something like that?"

"Half an hour before the paperwork arrived, Nephi was standing in front of the cigar counter asking me if I was going to pay him a pension when the building's gone."

"Not even Willis Tanner would hire Bates for a spy," Martin said.

"If a man keeps his ears open, he can hear a lot running an elevator."

Before Traveler could respond, Yancey came out of the men's room and continued his inspection of the lobby, making constant checkmarks on his clipboard. Finally, he stopped directly in front of the cigar stand and craned his neck to stare up at the massive mural that ran across the lobby's ceiling.

Chester retrieved a fresh cigar from the countertop, thrust it into the eternal flame, then fired smoke in Yancey's direction. Usually he asked strangers for permission to smoke, since tobacco was like brimstone to Mormons.

"That's old-fashioned, out of date, and faded." Yancey's face was pinched, whether from smoke or art criticism it was impossible to tell. "It makes the whole place as dark as a grotto. Give me whitewashed concrete any day."

"That's Brigham Young leading his pioneers to the promised land," Chester said.

"If you say so."

"It needs a little cleaning, that's all." Chester waved away his cigar smoke. "I've been meaning to get after it for years."

"This place smells like a train station," Yancey said.

Behind Yancey's back, Martin signaled Chester to get rid of the cigar. Chester made a face but did it, dousing it carefully so it could be relit later.

"It's a crime to let an eyesore like this continue to stand across the street from our temple," Yancey went on. "It's . . ." He stared up at the ceiling again as if seeking inspiration. ". . . disrespectful."

"Not so fast," Martin said. "That's a WPA mural up there, painted by Thomas Hart Benton. Isn't that right, Barney?"

"Absolutely. The man who built this place, old Gussie Gustavson, stood here and watched Tom Benton at work. He told me so himself."

Traveler leaned against the counter and looked up at the ceiling, seeking signs of Thomas Hart Benton, but knowing Barney had no proof as to who painted it, only word of mouth, Gussie Gustavson's word at that, which didn't stop the mural from being impressive despite a yellow patina caused by generations of cigar smoke. A line of wagons, prairie schooners, rolled across the ceiling, their sails caught in a wind that blew them westward. Men, women, and children walked beside their wagons; some carried infants, others led livestock, while Brigham Young rode on horseback at the head of the caravan. Behind him, snow-covered mountains and gigantic cumulus clouds served as a dramatic backdrop to the pioneer trek. The painter had made everyone and everything look bigger than life, though not big enough, Traveler thought, to convey the achievement itself, the Mormon migration that had crossed the Great Plains and the Rockies, fleeing murderous enemies, to reach their haven in Salt Lake City.

"Benton is a national treasure," Martin said.

Yancey squinted at Martin. "When was it painted?"

"The thirties, during the Great Depression."

"The painter's probably dead, then, and in no position to object—or sue, either, for that matter." Yancey made a notation on his clipboard. "I think I'll take a look at the second and third floors now."

"You don't need me with you, then," Chester said. "Besides, there's nothing up there to steal."

"Your elevator operator can accompany me."

"You must know Nephi Bates already, since he's a great one for the church too."

For a moment Yancey stood there, unmoving, then he shook his head once, slowly, and walked into the elevator whose brass grillwork matched the rest of the Chester Building's art deco styling.

Nephi Bates, whose earphones were around his neck, greeted the appraiser with a wary nod and then turned up the volume on the cassette player hooked to his belt. Immediately, the Mormon Tabernacle Choir's "Bringing in the Sheaves" began spilling out, the verses trailing off as the elevator rose out of sight:

"Sowing in the morning, sowing seeds of kindness,
Sowing in the noon-tide and the dewy eves;
Waiting for the harvest, and the time of reaping,
We shall come rejoicing, bringing in the sheaves."

Chester said, "I haven't got a chance unless you help me."

"You need a lawyer," Martin said, "not private detectives. What about Reed Critchlow? He's one of your oldest tenants."

"He's practically retired. Besides, we're up against the church here."

"You don't know that for sure," Traveler said.

"Let's say I'm hiring you to find out, then."

As soon as Chester turned away to relight his cigar in the eternal flame, Traveler and Martin exchanged knowing looks. They both knew the vacancy rate in the Chester Building was over fifty percent at the moment, so Chester couldn't afford an extensive investigation; they also knew they'd do their best to help him.

"Thank God for one thing," Martin said. "Drag your feet and eminent domain can take years."

Chester shook his head. "My hearing is in thirty days."

"Now we know what Willis meant on the phone," Traveler said.

"What's he got to do with this?" Chester asked.

"That boy knew about your building in advance," Martin said. "He told us not to ask him for help."

Chester bit through his cigar. "I'm finished, then. He speaks for the prophet."

"Willis didn't say he was speaking for anyone but himself," Traveler said.

Martin shook his head. "His motives are never clear, but

that doesn't change the fact that we may owe him one if his lead on my grandson works out."

"Whatever he is," Traveler said, "he isn't your grandson."

"If we raise him, he'll be as much your son as you are mine."

"Family comes first," Chester said. "I understand that."

Martin laid a hand on Chester's shoulder. "Mo and I will split up. I'll work on your problem while he goes to Park City to look for our namesake."

"Can I do anything to help?" Barney said.

"Check on Bill and Charlie. If bail's needed, Moroni Traveler and Son will chip in."

FOUR

Traveler drove east into the red-rock mouth of Parley's Canyon, named for the early Mormon apostle Parley P. Pratt, whose pioneer toll road was now I-80. The interstate wound its way through stands of birch, mountain alder, and big-tooth maples. At Kimball Junction, he turned south on State Highway 224, the route to Park City.

On Sunday drives when he was a boy, the high mountain meadows around Park City had been filled with chokecherry, quaking aspen, and yellowbelly marmots. Now there were ski runs, golf courses, and condominiums all the way into the heart of the old mining town, where more silver was being extracted from "old-time shopping days" than ever had been taken from its diggings. Main Street, with its weathered frame buildings on the verge of disintegration, had been carefully preserved for the tourists. In one of them, Dr. Giles Wilmot had his office.

Traveler parked in front of the old city hall, now a museum, and got out. At seven thousand feet, twenty-five hundred feet higher than Salt Lake City, the afternoon air was cold. The surrounding mountains were already tipped with snow; the opening of ski season was only a month away.

The sign on Wilmot's door gave office hours as nine to four twice a week, Wednesdays and Thursdays. Traveler checked his watch. He had thirty minutes to spare.

A cowbell attached to the door clanged loudly when he entered. He had to duck to avoid hitting his head on the pioneer-size door frame. The waiting room was empty except for a white-haired man of about seventy sitting in front of a low table covered with documents. He wore a starched lab coat and white shirt with a carefully knotted black knit tie.

"You cut it pretty close," he said, rising to shake hands. "I'm Dr. Wilmot. When Willis Tanner called me, he predicted you'd be here an hour ago."

"What else did he say?"

"He asked me to give you a hand." The man's tone said he might not have done so otherwise.

"I understand you've found another Moroni Traveler."

Wilmot gestured at the papers on the table. "For the past year I've been going over every record I could get hold of here in town, marriages, deaths, baptisms, deeds, you name it. I've walked the cemetery and recorded every tombstone myself. Do you know why?"

Traveler knew better than to answer; he merely shook his head as was expected of him.

"California money is pouring in here, that's why. It's erasing our history. Gentile money. It's worse than the fire of 1898 that nearly wiped us out. Back then we rebuilt the town. Now they're rebuilding the mountains to make the skiing better. Soon there won't be anything left of Park City the way it was. Nobody to remember it either. That's where I come in."

Traveler bent over the table hoping to spot some reference to Moroni the Third.

Wilmot immediately reassembled the papers into a single pile with a face-down page on top. "Did you know that Park

City was originally named Upper Kimballs, after the ranch of the same name? Some called it Upper Parleys for the apostle Parley Pratt, who built a toll road up from Salt Lake."

Traveler sighed.

"Of course you didn't. That's why I'm collecting everything I can. Every name, every soul has to be accounted for. You must know that, being named for our angel the way you are."

"I'm interested in genealogy," Traveler said. Unspoken was the Mormon belief that all ancestors had to be researched and documented and then raised from the dead one at a time during a temple baptism.

The doctor removed a pair of wire-rimmed glasses from his breast pocket, donned them carefully, and stared at Traveler as if attempting to assess his sincerity.

"I have a son your age," he said finally. "He played for West High School when you played for East. You beat us three years straight. That shouldn't have happened. East was a rich kids' school."

"We lived on the Avenues," Traveler said. "Not Federal Heights."

"My wife, rest her soul, always wanted me to start up a regular practice and move to the Heights. But I told her, 'There's work here in the mines that has to be done.' So she and my boy stayed on in my father's house on the west side, the wrong side of the tracks, forcing me to commute. 'You don't have sense enough to see the mines are dying,' she used to say to me. My only regret is she never did get the new home she dreamed about."

Wilmot squinted at Traveler for a while, then removed his glasses and tossed them on the table. "My son said you were the best he ever played against. He said you played like a crazy man. Even so, West would have kicked your ass if it hadn't been for that last-minute fumble."

Traveler remembered the fumble, the game too, hard-fought and vicious, but no opposing player named Wilmot.

"We followed your career in the pros. We kept waiting for you to get your ass kicked."

"I retired early," Traveler said.

"My son's a bishop now."

"I'm sure that's better than playing football."

"Maybe you can mention his name to Mr. Tanner. Bill Wilmot, bishop of the Cottonwood Ward."

"I'm sure Willis knows about him already, but I'll put in a good word. Now, can we get back to that namesake of mine."

The doctor stood up. "Come over to the window with me, Mr. Traveler, and tell me what you see."

Traveler followed but said nothing.

"It's a California movie set with actors instead of real people," Wilmot said. "My people are living in the alleys off Main Street, in the run-down cabins on the hillside that tourists think so quaint. My people are asphyxiating themselves in wintertime trying to stay warm with oil heaters, trying to hang on until God calls them home. When that happens, all that will be left is the actors, pretending to be pioneers."

The thought crossed Traveler's mind that Wilmot might be an actor too, playing a part written and directed by Willis Tanner.

"How did you know I was looking for Moroni Traveler?" Traveler asked.

"The word went out to account for all Moronis. It was the last thing I expected to find here, a child named for an angel in a town full of Gentile money."

Wilmot began whistling a tune Traveler didn't recognize. After a moment he switched to words.

> "Willie, oh Willie, go and dig my grave,
> Dig it wide and deep.
> Place the prayer book at my head,
> And the hymn book at my feet."

The doctor knocked on the side of his head with a knuckle. "You get to be my age, young man, you start losing your train of thought. So, before I forget altogether, it was Grandma Mabey's husband, old Eli, who told me about the child.

Strange now that I think about it. We never called him Grandpa, just old Eli or old Mabey. The man's ninety now, maybe more."

"How does he know about the child?" Traveler asked.

"What with Mr. Tanner being involved, it's probably best you don't get it secondhand."

FIVE

Eli Mabey lived in a one-room relic that looked more like a clapboard lean-to than a house. It couldn't have been more than ten feet wide, with a single window and a narrow unpainted door facing Empire Avenue, two blocks off the main drag and well out of sight of the skiers' condominiums. A metal stovepipe protruded from one weatherbeaten wall and rose precariously above a disintegrating shingle roof. A low picket fence, gray with age and missing most of its stakes, surrounded the tiny, weed-filled yard. The ramshackle gate came off in Dr. Wilmot's hand.

"Like I told you, Park City all but burned to the ground around the turn of the century." Wilmot dropped the gate in the undergrowth and headed for the door. "Old Mabey says this place escaped because the flames refused to take it."

At his knock a voice rasped, "It's open, ferchrissake, like always."

"I'm just giving you a chance to get decent," Wilmot called back.

"It's okay to come in. I've hidden the women and doused my cigarettes."

Traveler had to stoop to follow the doctor inside. The room contained a narrow rumpled cot, a chest of drawers, a pioneer pie safe with perforated tin doors, a metal kitchen table, and an assortment of mismatched chairs, only one of which had enough upholstery to look comfortable. Eli Mabey stood beside that one, holding on to the chair's back for support with one hand, his aluminum walker with the other. He was wearing a faded flannel shirt and baggy tan slacks. Cigarette smoke hung in the air above his head. Traveler saw no sign of an ashtray, though the door to an unlit iron stove stood open.

"Here's the visitor I promised you," the doctor said.

"I'm not blind yet," Mabey replied.

"Moroni Traveler," the doctor clarified.

"He's too small to be an angel and too big to stand there bent over like that. Light somewhere so I don't have to kink my neck looking up at you."

Traveler crossed the ragged linoleum that had once been patterned to resemble an Oriental rug and sat on a folding metal chair within spitting distance of the stove.

"I can smell cigarette smoke," Wilmot said.

"The place must be on fire, then."

"You're going to kill yourself one of these days, Eli."

"God, I hope so."

"I'll leave you here, Traveler," Wilmot said. "I have other, more appreciative patients to see."

"He's like an old dog sniffing out sins." Mabey clicked his false teeth before maneuvering himself back into the overstuffed chair.

The doctor shook his head and left.

Mabey said, "You being named for an angel, I guess you wouldn't have a cigarette on you, would you?"

"I don't smoke," Traveler said, "and I was named for my father."

Sighing, Mabey fished a can of Copenhagen tobacco from his shirt pocket and slipped a pinch into his mouth. "What did the doc tell you about me?"

"Only that you could help me find a child named Moroni."

"He must be getting old, then. Usually, he makes everyone promise to sell me on the comfort of living in an old-folks' home." Mabey snorted. "You know what I tell them, don't you? Maybe. Maybe I'm going to move, maybe I'm not. Eli Mabey's famous for his maybes."

He winked before using a stained finger to probe his mouth for stray crumbs of tobacco. "Do you want to hear my life story?"

"I'd rather hear about Moroni."

Mabey grinned. "I got my first job here in Park City when I was fifteen. I was a powder monkey in the old Annie Lode mine. That's when I started smoking. It was against regulations, of course, that's why I did it. 'You're going to get us killed,' the boys used to say. 'Maybe, maybe not,' I'd tell them. Hell, I never worried a lick. I left that up to God. When I got married I left the praying to my wife, Naomi. You wouldn't know it to look at this place, but we had a good life here. It didn't look like this when she was alive, I can tell you. It was spit and polish and new curtains every other year."

At the moment, grime on the windowpanes provided the only privacy.

"Now they want to tear this whole section down and put up what they call time-shares for the winter people who come in from California for the skiing." Mabey shook his head. "Well, sir, I'll tell you the same thing I told the others. Naomi wouldn't want me selling out. That's why I'm not leaving this place till they carry me out."

His tongue probed his cheek for a moment. "You see that pie safe next to the sink? That's where I keep Naomi's things, right down to the last set of curtains she made. They're going to be buried with me, by God. Are you sure you haven't got any cigarettes?"

"I'll be glad to go out and buy you some if you're out."

"I'm not fool enough to run out, but it's hell when a man gets to be so old he can't do his own shopping. The ladies from the church Relief Society come in every other day, but they refuse to bring me my cigarettes. 'When you've lived as long as

I have,' I tell them, 'the Word of Wisdom doesn't count for much.' I read somewhere that Joseph Smith used to chew tobacco till his wife gave him hell for causing a mess. After that, he had a revelation and came up with the Word of Wisdom. Tell that to the Relief ladies, though, and they start reading the scripture to you till you wish you was deaf. 'Maybe I'll quit,' I say, just to get rid of them. 'Maybe, maybe.' There's not much they can do to you when you're my age. Hell, if Joe Smith himself walked in here right now, I'd offer him a chew. Come to think of it, what about you?"

Mabey brought out his Copenhagen again. "Don't worry about taking my last wad. I've got another can stashed in with Naomi's things. That's one place the Reliefers know better than to snoop."

Traveler shook his head.

"I'll use your share to reload, then. While you're at it, hand me that can on the stove."

The coffee can smelled like a spittoon, which was exactly what Mabey used it for. When he spit into it, tobacco juice ran down his chin, reaching his neck before he wiped it on his sleeve.

"You can't spit in front of the Relief ladies, not and feel right about it. Besides, they report everything I do to Doc Wilmot. The old boy couldn't make it these days, you know, what with the ski people wanting fancy doctors who've got nothing better to do but sit around and wait for some darn fool to break a leg, so they can slap on one of them walking casts and charge a mint. If you broke a leg in my day, the doc gave you a slug of whiskey and told Joe Smith to look the other way if he didn't like it. After that, the doc yanked your bones back into place and sent you on your way."

He gestured toward the window. "Take a look outside. I'll bet the doc's out there right now, pacing back and forth and wondering if you're helping me go to hell by smoking cigarettes."

Traveler obliged. "He's out there, all right." Only Wilmot

wasn't pacing, he was trying to repair the broken gate. "Tell me what brand you smoke and I'll pick you up a carton."

"Moyle's Market is the closest. Two blocks down and one over." Mabey brought the can close to his mouth to avoid dribbling on himself. "To think it's come to this after seventy years of smoking. Take my advice, son. A man should die before his legs give out. The trouble is, God keeps us waiting, doesn't he? Or maybe it's the other way around. Maybe. That's life. One maybe after another."

He squinted at Traveler, who was leaning against the wall next to the window. "Speaking of God, you don't look like you ought to be named for an angel."

"It's a family name."

"Our relatives load us down, don't they, with all their baggage passed on from one generation to another. That's why I smoke Camels, just like my father. The short ones, too. Real coffin nails. That's what Naomi used to call 'em. She's been gone a long time. I was an old man even then. The older you get, the more folks shy away from you, especially the young ones. They don't want to be reminded of what's to come."

He plucked a loose cigarette from his shirt pocket, struck a kitchen match with his thumbnail, and lit up. The cigarette, Traveler noticed, had a filter tip and smelled mentholated.

"Where was I?" Mabey said.

"A child named Moroni."

"Not so fast. It's not every day I get a visitor. I get the Relief ladies all right, but they don't say much. Mostly they pray. Doc Wilmot's gabby at times, but only because he knows I'm due to be called home anytime now. That's why he hangs around us old gazoonies, taking down our histories on that tape recorder of his. Questions about the old days, that's all he asks. Hell, I make up stories just to have someone to talk to. Of course, Doc's starting to catch on, looking bored most of the time. But he sure perked up when I mentioned my old friend Glen Bosworth, whose daughter had a late-life kid."

He paused to take a long drag on his cigarette. After exhaling, he leaned back and closed his eyes. "You guessed it, the kid was named Moroni."

Mabey went back to his cigarette, sucking on it until there was nothing left but filter. Then he dropped it into the spittoon, where it died with a hiss.

"Yes, sir. It's hard to imagine an angel's name in the Bosworth family, what with them never setting foot inside a church as far as I know."

"How long ago was the child born?"

Mabey's fingers dipped into his shirt pocket again and came up with another cigarette. Instead of lighting up, he rolled it between his fingers. "My memory's not what it used to be, except when it comes to the old days. But it must have been three years ago."

Until that moment Traveler had been expecting failure, another of Claire's games played on him all the way from her grave. But three years made the timing right. Three years ago, she'd claimed to have given away Moroni Traveler the Third.

"I'll need the mother's name," he said. "Her married name."

Mabey tucked the cigarette, now leaking shreds of tobacco from its business end, behind his ear. "Come to think of it, maybe I never knew. Maybe I never paid much attention. Maybe I'm getting senile. Maybe."

"Maybe," Traveler said, "the child was adopted?"

Mabey shook his head. "Glen never said anything about that. Me and him go way back, too, to the days when they were still taking ore out of the Annie Lode. You should have seen us then. You should have seen this town. It was booming. Saloons everywhere, filled with redheaded women. We thought we were rich. Of course, the real money went to the mine owners. Doc was one of the last company doctors, you know. There was those who said he wasn't much of a doctor, that it was the only job he could get, but he took good care of us just the same. If you were laid up, not working and not getting paid, the price of your medicine came out of the doc's pocket often as not. Not that he'd admit it."

"You were talking about Moroni?" Traveler said.

"Anyone named for an angel working the mine in my day would have got the shit beat out of him. Though come to think of it, you look big enough to take care of yourself. Old Glen would have taken you on, though. In his prime, that man loved a good fight."

"Maybe I could meet him."

"Didn't I say? Glen's been called home, he and his missis both. By then they were long gone from here, of course, living out in Bingham with his daughter and her husband, who wanted to try his hand working for Kennecott Copper. When it came to his family, Glen should have had more sense. Take me and my missis. We sent our two boys away from the mines the first chance we got. Right now, they're both living the good life in California. They keep asking me to come stay with them, but I know better. Besides, you know what they say about old dogs."

He removed the cigarette from behind his ear and ran it under his nose before lighting up. "The last time I saw Glen, his daughter drove him up here to see me and show off the grandkid. His lungs were giving out even then. I suppose that's what's going to get me, too, all that mine dust."

Mabey paused to inhale deeply.

"Is the daughter still in Bingham?"

"Maybe."

"It would help to have her married name," Traveler said.

"Didn't you ask me about that already?"

"Maybe."

Eli Mabey grinned. "Her name has nothing to do with an angel, that's for sure."

He dropped his cigarette into the coffee can and sloshed it around. "That was my last coffin nail, young man."

"Do you think your memory will improve if I come back with a carton or two?"

"Maybe."

SIX

The rising tide of California money hadn't yet reached Moyle's Market. The building, not much bigger than Eli Mabey's lean-to house, was made of rough rock-faced oolite that had weathered to the color of old asphalt. The windows, deep-set into the rock, reminded Traveler of a jail; the metal door looked like salvage from a gas station. A faded sign hanging from the flat roof said O. W. MOYLE PROP.

Stepping inside was like reentering childhood, back in Affleck's Grocery on T Street where Traveler and Willis Tanner had spent their allowances on Hostess Cupcakes and RC Colas—twelve ounces, double the size of Coke—and Baby Ruths and Bit-O'-Honeys. Even the wooden floor was the same, as was the sharp sawdust smell, and the cigarette display, high up on the wall behind the counter, well out of reach to minors, with a notice saying ID REQUIRED.

"A carton of Camels," Traveler told the young woman behind the counter wearing the kind of stiffly sprayed beehive hairdo he hadn't seen in years.

She arched an eyebrow that didn't match her hair color.

"One look at you tells me old Mabey's roped in another one."

Traveler took two twenties from his wallet and laid them on the counter.

"It never fails," she said. "People go up to the old boy's place, listen to those stories of his, which he makes up if you ask me, and then come down here doing their best to kill him off." She dog-eared the paperback she was reading and laid it on the fly-littered window ledge behind her. "He wants short ones to boot, Camels, not even filter tips. Coffin nails, Doc Wilmot calls them."

Traveler felt as guilty as he had when he and Willis used to buy cigarettes when they were underage. The Union Pacific Depot was their favorite place, since passengers seldom got asked for their ID.

"We send him up one pack a day," the woman went on. "Those are Doc Wilmot's orders. That's Mabey's limit, he says. 'Anyone caught sneaking him in more than that will have to answer to me.' The doc's very words."

"He told me he wouldn't talk anymore until I showed some good faith," Traveler said.

"It's a bluff. He does it all the time. He knows he'll have to settle for ice cream, low-fat at that. If it's all the same to you, we'll use your money to pay for strawberry, his favorite."

Traveler nodded and left the twenties where they were.

"That'll keep him supplied for the next couple of months. You can take up a carton of strawberry yourself, if you want to. Better you than me. I'm tired of getting my ears talked off."

"I'd like to make a phone call first," Traveler said.

"It's on the wall in the back next to the milk case."

The wall was covered with jottings, phone numbers mostly, and one riddle, which Traveler remembered from high school. WHAT'S PURPLE AND HAS TWENTY-SEVEN WIVES? BRIGHAM PLUM.

He picked up the receiver, dialed Moroni Traveler and Son, and got a busy signal. After a few moments, he tried again but the line was still busy.

Sighing, he went back to the front counter and paid for his

———————

Hostess Cupcakes and a Diet Coke. "Do you want me to eat this outside?"

The woman shrugged. "Why bother? No one else does."

He took his snack back to the phone and tasted memories for a while. As soon as the recollections subsided, he began wondering what the hell he was doing in Park City, looking for a child that wasn't even his. A child who, even if he existed, was someone else's son by now.

Chances were old Eli Mabey had made a mistake. Even if he hadn't, the Moroni in question was probably just what Eli said, a late-life child. Nothing to do with Claire.

Haven't you learned by now? he asked himself. Claire's still pulling your strings.

I loved playing puppets as a child, she'd said to him once. *I'd control their every move. I'd sing to them and make them dance. I'd put words in their mouths and make them fight.*

That admission had come after she'd orchestrated a fistfight for him, one where he was outnumbered. Traveler brushed his shoulder, half expecting to feel that her strings were still attached.

They'd been out for a drive, sunbathing at Black Rock on the Great Salt Lake until Claire caught sight of sewage floating in the water.

"They say the salt kills everything," Traveler had reassured her, but she wanted to leave.

Rather than head back to town, they'd taken State Highway 36 south through the towns of Toole, Vernon, and then Eureka, an old mining center with more historic buildings left than people. From Eureka, they doubled back on Highway 6 to Goshen, which had a history of name changes, from Sodom to Sandtown to Mechanicsville.

There, Claire insisted on stopping for lunch at the Tintic Bar and Grill, named for the Ute Indian chief who carried on bloody guerrilla warfare against the Mormon pioneers. If it hadn't been for the lighted neon COORS sign out front, the place would have looked derelict.

The expression on Claire's face should have warned him to

keep on driving, but he was thinking of how good a hamburger and a cold beer would taste. By the time they were inside the crowded bar it was too late.

"Claire," the bartender shouted, "we haven't seen you in a dog's age. If you're looking for LaVar, he's shooting pool in the back room."

Claire shook her head, a show gesture judging by the look in her eyes; it was meant to appease Traveler but also to let him know she was in demand. There would be no getting out of there without seeing LaVar, he knew that immediately.

"We just stopped in for lunch," she said.

The bartender eyed Traveler. "Give me your order, and I'll bring it to your table."

"You know what I like," Claire said.

"Ribs it is. What about you, pal?"

"Make it two." As soon as the bartender had handed over a pitcher of beer and two glasses, Traveler led the way to a table where he could keep his back to the wall.

"How do you happen to know this place?" he asked as soon as Claire was seated.

"It's from one of my previous lives. The land of Goshen. Don't you just love it?"

"And LaVar?"

"He could have escaped to the big city, but he chose not to."

"With you?"

"You know the rules, Moroni. Past lives don't count."

The man who brought the ribs set them on the table with an exaggerated bow. He looked like a cowboy, tall, lanky, with a sun-leathered face and hands.

"Mo, meet LaVar," Claire said.

When Traveler stood up to shake hands, LaVar's eyes widened. "You're a big bastard, aren't you?"

The man's cowboy boots, Traveler realized, made him look taller than he was, no more than five-eight. He had to crane his neck to look Traveler in the face. He tried to turn the handshake into a contest, but Traveler decided not to play.

"Claire always said I was big where it counts," LaVar said with a wink.

"This is Moroni Traveler," Claire added.

"Christ, she left me for an angel." LaVar raised his voice. "Do you hear that! This guy's named Moroni."

"Hell, yes," the bartender said, pounding the bartop. "I recognize him now. He played in the pros, linebacker for L.A. One mean muther."

"He looks like a twangy boy to me," LaVar said.

"Claire," Traveler said. "We can still walk out of here."

She licked her lips. "I haven't eaten yet."

"You back off, LaVar," the bartender said.

"This ain't no ballgame." LaVar jerked a thumb over his shoulder. "Besides, I got friends backing me up."

The dozen men at the bar stopped talking to watch. Traveler sat down, hoping that would give LaVar some sense of victory.

"Menlove," Claire said softly.

Traveler fingered a french fry.

"That's LaVar's last name," she clarified. "Men-love."

LaVar glared. "What's that supposed to mean?"

"Men love," she said. "Loves men." In the silence Claire's voice carried throughout the barroom.

"Bitch," LaVar said.

"Moroni," Claire said, wheedling.

LaVar's eyes widened. Maybe he was seeing the light; maybe he'd back off.

"You don't have to be jealous, Moroni," Claire said. "LaVar never did have any lead in his pencil, except in the men's locker room."

Traveler shook his head against the memory of the fight that had followed. The remembered taste of blood subsided, overridden by the cupcake's residue.

He drank the last of his Coke and phoned his father again. This time the line was free.

"There's another Moroni, all right," Traveler said. "Living out in Bingham Canyon somewhere. I haven't got the family name yet, so I'll stick around here for a while."

"I need your help here. Barney's going crazy. He can't find Bill and Charlie."

"They were supposed to be under arrest."

"The police say they escaped from the hospital right after Bill had his leg set."

"On crutches?"

"I'm just telling you what they told Barney when he showed up with a bail bondsman. Bill and Charlie are now considered fugitives."

"I don't like the sound of that," Traveler said.

"Neither did the bail bondsman. He told Barney the last time something like that happened, the police were trying to cover up a beating."

"What do you think?"

"That Bill should have known better than to mess around with the White Prophet."

"The man's only an apostle, and all Bill tried to do was touch him."

"Barney says it's part of the conspiracy against him and his building. He says the church has spirited Bill and Charlie away because they're his friends. He says we'll be the next to disappear, leaving him to face the church alone."

"You sound like you believe him," Traveler said.

"You never know."

Dr. Wilmot was waiting outside Moyle's Market, leaning against the rusted door of a pickup that would have looked abandoned except for the up-to-date state inspection sticker on its windshield.

"I spoke with old Eli after you left him," Wilmot said. "He tells me you're looking for Glen Bosworth's daughter, so I figured I'd put a word in your ear about that."

"I'm on my way to deliver Eli's ice cream."

Wilmot waved away the comment. "I've doctored a lot of men in my time, enough to tell me more than I want to know about human nature. Take a man like yourself. I might be able to make a good guess why you're looking for a namesake, but I won't. That's your business. Keeping my patients healthy is mine. Sometimes outsiders, people like you, don't make that easy. I'm not talking about the cigarettes only. Eli can be very persuasive. But Moyle's knows better than to deliver more than I prescribe." He paused for breath. "I'm talking about you personally. You're the kind who keeps pushing until something gives. I don't want that something to be Eli Mabey."

"All I want is a name," Traveler said.

"That's why I'm standing here when I have better things to do. I intend to point you in the right direction, so you won't have to bother Eli with any more damn fool questions. The woman you're looking for is Hannah Tempest. She and her sister are both living in Bingham, though for how long I don't know, since Kennecott is looking to buy the place."

"Did you deliver Mrs. Tempest's child?"

"I don't talk about my patients, Mr. Traveler, even after they've moved away."

SEVEN

An hour later, Traveler parked in a loading zone in front of the Chester Building. Nightfall had brought with it a warm wind, smelling of sycamores, mountain sage, and the promise of rain. Across the street, the floodlit temple rose like a Gothic beacon, its two-hundred-foot spires visible throughout the valley.

Traveler had half expected Martin to be waiting on the sidewalk so they could head directly for the police station. Instead, he was behind the cigar stand, serving coffee to Barney Chester and his elevator operator, Nephi Bates. Usually Chester allowed no one but himself behind the counter. At the moment, he looked slump-shouldered and dispirited. His hair was uncombed, his unlit cigar limp and on the verge of disintegration.

Bates looked as he always did, prim, his cassette player hooked into his belt, the earphones slung around his neck.

"It's Mormon coffee," Bates explained, extending his cup at Traveler's approach. "Hot water with cream and sugar."

"I used to give it to Moroni as a boy," Martin said. "He always wanted what the rest of us were drinking, so we told him it was coffee. He never knew the difference."

"I knew," Traveler said.

"Your mother said cream and sugar took the sin out of coffee. What do you say to that, Brother Nephi?"

Bates eyed his cup. "A man needs all the friends he can get at a time like this."

"Nephi's been trying to help us," Chester said. "Not that it will do any good. You can't fight the church, not in this state."

Bates set his cup on the countertop. "When I first heard about the plans for the Chester Building, it sounded like God's work. So I said to myself, 'Nephi,' I said, 'you can't think about yourself when God needs more room, when he needs a parking lot for his house across the street.' "

"Would you like some coffee, Moroni?" Martin said, raising an eyebrow to indicate that he had real coffee in mind, or maybe that Bates's Mormon coffee wasn't as sin-free as the elevator operator had claimed.

Traveler accepted a cup without comment.

"The church takes care of its own," Bates went on. "I've always heard that."

"They promised him another job," Martin explained.

"A man my age doesn't like change." Bates took his pocket-size edition of *The Book of Mormon* and held it tightly in both hands.

" 'And he that live in righteousness shall be changed in the twinkling of an eye, and the earth shall pass away so as by fire,' " Martin quoted.

Nodding, Bates walked the dozen or so paces to his elevator, where he ran his hand over the operating lever. "There are no more jobs for the likes of me. Not like this. This is the last of the great elevators here in Zion. Nowadays they're nothing but metal boxes with buttons to push, with no need for an old man like me. When I thought on that, I said to myself, 'Nephi,' I said, 'surely God would not want a work of art like this to be lost.' "

He left the elevator and returned to the cigar counter.

"You'll always have a job with me, Nephi." Chester's words carried with them the smell of alcohol. Traveler tested his coffee and found it laced heavily with brandy.

"If I have to," Chester went on, "I'll find you another place."

Bates's chin sank onto his breastbone. "I don't want charity."

"There are plenty of old buildings left in this town."

"They've all been modernized," Bates said. His breath seemed to smell of brandy too, or was Traveler mistaken?

"Maybe I've let this place go too long," Chester said. "When you think about it, there are plenty of things that need doing around here. Maybe if we work together, Nephi, you and I, we can make the old girl so beautiful no one would dare touch her. Are you game?"

The elevator operator raised his head.

"Are you afraid of heights, Nephi?" Chester pointed at the lobby's ceiling. "If not, the two of us can go to work cleaning the mural up there."

Bates stared up at Brigham Young and his band of pioneers. "For a minute there, I thought maybe we could do it, Mr. Chester. But you won't have a building soon, or a ceiling to clean either."

"Don't you believe it," Martin said. "Moroni Traveler and Son has been housed here thirty years. That's why we've promised to fight this thing."

"But we can't do it without your help, Nephi," Traveler added. "That's why you have to tell us what you heard about the building."

When Bates lowered his gaze, his eyes were glistening with tears. "He said it was a church matter. That means God must have spoken to the prophet."

"I don't think God talks about real estate," Martin said.

Bates's eyes went wide; he blinked and backed up a step as if to disassociate himself with possible blasphemy.

"If they want the Chester Building for a parking lot," Martin persisted, "it has nothing to do with God."

Bates pressed his lips into a tight line and folded his arms across his chest, the picture of a man intending to remain mute.

"Nephi," Martin wheedled.

Bates shook his head.

"So be it," Traveler said. "Come on, Dad, we still have time to see the police before dinner."

"They were talking right in front of me," Bates blurted. "Like I didn't exist. Like I was deaf and dumb, just part of the elevator. It was the day you were out of town, Mr. Chester. You were out of your office too, Mr. Traveler, both you and your father."

"There you have it, then," Martin said. "You weren't sworn to silence."

"Mr. Tanner speaks for the prophet. You know that." Awe filled Bates's voice.

"Most likely he was speaking for himself," Martin said. "Besides, eminent domain is the province of government, not religion."

"Technically correct," Chester said, "but where are you going to find a judge and jury in this state who'll say no to the church?"

Bates closed his eyes. "Mr. Tanner says the Chester Building is only the beginning. He envisions—that was his word—an entire square block designed to complement the temple. He said the new church office building up the street had been a mistake, because it's taller than the temple. Therefore, a new look is needed. I remember his exact words. 'The temple must be resurrected in a new setting of proper grandeur.' "

"Who was he saying all this to?" Traveler asked.

"The thirteenth apostle."

Martin shook his head. "White Prophets and thirteenth apostles are too much for me on an empty stomach. I'm going to dinner and then home to bed."

"What about Bill and Charlie?" Traveler said.

"Chances are we're not going to get anything accomplished until we can backtrack them in daylight."

"What do we do about Willis?" Chester said.

"He's on his honeymoon," Martin said. "And we're sure as hell not going to get in to see the thirteenth apostle until business hours tomorrow."

EIGHT

Martin insisted on leaving the house at eight o'clock the next morning. Even that early, the temperature was seventy degrees.

While Traveler drove, Martin switched on the car radio. According to forecasters, the unseasonable weather was expected to last for another twenty-four hours, thanks to a high-pressure system centered over the Great Salt Lake Basin. By the time they'd driven half a mile, the radio in Traveler's Ford Fairlane had warmed up enough to begin producing its usual static.

Martin pounded the dashboard. "When are you going to get rid of this piece of junk?"

"It's inconspicuous."

"Ugly's the word. Pull over to the curb."

As soon as the car stopped, Martin began fiddling with wires under the dashboard. They'd come to a halt in front of the Wasatch School, which Traveler had attended through the seventh grade.

"This radio's old enough to have tubes," Martin said.

Across the street, students were filing into the tunnel that allowed them to cross under South Temple without having to worry about traffic. Their ritual shouts—to ward off creatures said to lurk underground—echoed just as hollowly as they had in Traveler's time.

"Henry Ford has a lot to answer for," Martin muttered.

"We could always go back home and get your Jeep."

"Iacocca's no better." Martin sat up and began wiping his hands on his handkerchief. "A man my age needs a little music in the morning to soothe his nerves."

"I'll buy a new radio."

"It's a wonder this car passes inspection."

Traveler pulled away from the curb and headed downtown. The Ford, years beyond its prime, was the kind of disreputable relic Martin had driven when Traveler was a boy.

"Do you remember the old Packard?" Traveler said.

"A great car. Your mother hated it."

"She didn't like being seen in it, especially on Sunday drives."

"She was a great one for putting on the dog."

By the time Traveler turned south on Second East, he'd attracted a patrol car. No flashing lights came on, but it was definitely following them.

"I can't see who's driving," he said.

Martin released his seat belt so he could turn around in the bucket seat. "The sun's in my eyes, but considering our destination, I'm betting on Anson Horne. The man thinks he's Defender of the Faith against Gentiles like us."

"How could he know where we're going?"

"You're forgetting Nephi Bates. For all we know, he's an agent provocateur."

"Now that he's about to lose his job, the man's acting like a human being for once. Brace yourself." Traveler hit the brakes. Behind him, the patrol car did the same, coming to a stop in a spot of shade that allowed Traveler to see Horne behind the wheel.

"So let him follow us," Martin said. "This early we ought to be able to park right in front of the apostle's place of business. That ought to give Horne something to think about."

Traveler turned right on Second South, continuing as far as West Temple. From there, three more right turns brought him around the block on the same side of Main Street as the Kearns Building, where the man known as the thirteenth apostle had his offices.

Anson Horne's car closed the gap to park behind them. The policeman got out immediately and motioned Traveler and Martin to join him on the sidewalk. His partner, Earl Belnap, stayed in the car, glaring at them.

Horne said, "I'm looking for Boyd Williams."

Traveler smiled. It had been a long time since he'd heard Boyd called anything but Mad Bill or the Sandwich Prophet.

"You saved us a trip to the police station to ask you where Bill's gotten to," Martin said.

"You know damn well he's a fugitive. He and that Indian of his."

"The last time we saw them," Traveler said, "they were with you."

"If either of them contacts you, I want to know about it."

"Do you think I'm hiding them in the trunk of the car?" Traveler said.

Horne jerked his head in Belnap's direction. The man immediately got out of the patrol car, took Traveler's keys, and opened the Ford's trunk.

"How did Bill manage to escape with a cast on his leg?" Traveler asked.

Belnap slammed the trunk lid, leaving the keys dangling in the lock. At a nod from Horne, the sergeant got back in the patrol car.

"You know how it is with hospitals," Horne said. "There's a lot of paperwork to do. I turned my back for a minute and they were gone."

"Where was your partner?"

"I've never lost a prisoner before, so as far as I'm concerned this is personal."

Martin stared at Horne, who was solidly built, the same muscled width from shoulders to waist. "Why would Bill risk additional charges by attempting to escape? As it stood, all you had against him was trespassing."

"He damaged church property," Horne said.

"He stepped on a few flowers and waded in the seagull pool."

"He assaulted an apostle."

"He only wanted to touch the man," Traveler said.

"For all Josiah Ellsworth knew, he was being attacked by apostates."

"Has he filed charges?" Traveler said.

"That hasn't been decided yet."

"Bill and Charlie aren't dangerous," Martin said, "you know that. They can't escape for long either, not with you and the church looking for them."

"This is strictly a temporal matter," Horne said. "At the moment."

Traveler didn't like the sound of that. "What do you know about the Chester Building?"

"We know those two live in the basement there, if that's what you mean."

"Don't try using them as leverage against us," Traveler said.

Horne lowered his voice. "Just find them. Otherwise, I won't be responsible." He stalked away, forcing Belnap to drive down Main Street after him.

Traveler shook his head and stared up at the Kearns Building. For a moment he thought he saw a silhouette against the skyline ten stories above. Rubbing his eyes brought only blue sky into focus.

"I saw him too," Martin said.

"Who?"

"There's a story about Sam Howe. They say he's everywhere. They say he sees everything and knows all the secrets. As church lawyer, he keeps them too. Even so, he's still an unofficial apostle, still number thirteen. Of course, he wasn't born into the church; he's a convert."

Traveler craned his neck for a second look. The building had been constructed in 1911 for Thomas Kearns, one of the mining millionaires who came out of Park City in the 1880s. Its reinforced concrete was a marvel of the time, as was a design hinting at Renaissance revival that included a facing of white terra-cotta tile and boldly projecting cornices at the roof line.

"His offices take up the entire top floor," Martin went on. "The perfect spot to keep an eye on things."

"Next you'll be telling me he's got second sight."

"I've heard that said about him, too."

"Remind me to tell him that old Tom Kearns was a Catholic."

"I hear they exorcised the whole top floor before Howe moved in."

Going up in the elevator, Traveler remembered that Kearns, like his building, had become an icon in Utah. Although Catholic, he served one term in the United States Senate, taking office at the turn of the century, a time when a kind of gentlemen's agreement existed between Gentiles and the church. One senator would be Mormon, the church decreed, the other would be a Gentile, a policy derived to placate Mormon-baiters in Washington. These days, the church had no such qualms.

At the tenth floor, the elevator doors opened directly onto a foyer carpeted with amber-colored chenille overlaid with Oriental rugs. Along the walls, free-standing copper torchier lamps with mica shades cast pools of soft golden light onto the trowel-marked stucco ceiling. A single desk with its own smaller beaten-copper lamp stood in front of a walnut door, the foyer's only visible exit. The woman behind the desk, wearing a dark brown suit with a blouse that matched the amber carpet, rose to greet them.

"Mr. Howe is expecting you," she said.

Martin insisted on handing her a business card.

"Moroni Traveler and Son," she said without looking at it.

Traveler and Martin exchanged wary looks before following her through the doorway. The room beyond, an antechamber, was furnished as a waiting area, with pioneer sofa benches and armchairs so perfect they might have been expensive reproductions. Theater-size copper wall sconces, fitted with mica louvers, provided subdued amber light.

The secretary paused in front of a large east-facing window and looked out at the Wasatch Mountains as if expecting Traveler and Martin to do the same. Her hesitation, Traveler thought, looked practiced. Her posture, even the placement of her low-heeled shoes, was that of a fashion model.

"We are blessed," she said, "living here in the land of Zion, where God sent his chosen people."

Behind her back, Martin raised an eyebrow. She was preparing them, like an understudy warming up an audience for the main act.

Traveler moved close to the window. From such a vantage point, the eleven-thousand-foot glaciered peaks of the Wasatch reminded him of the crusted jaws of some fossil carnivore. Brigham Young, fleeing from religious persecution, had crossed those heights at the head of a wagon train in 1847. For years afterward, the Wasatch had served as a wall against his eastern enemies. To the west lay another vast barrier, the Great Salt Lake. Between the two of them, Brigham built his city of Zion. His glory, the faithful called it, a town laid out according to holy logic, with all life radiating out from its spiritual hub, the temple. Even the street names were part of his solemn master plan. Those directly adjacent to the temple were named East Temple, North Temple, West Temple, and South Temple. Farther out were the lettered and numbered streets and avenues, a rational progression all the way to the city limits. But recent years had brought with them the secular chaos of progress, until now Brigham's city was called Greater Salt Lake, with over a million people and everything that went with them.

"Mr. Howe is ready for you now," the secretary said. She smiled, secure in a job well done, and opened another hand-rubbed walnut door.

This time she didn't accompany them, but waited for them to pass through before closing the door behind them. Sam Howe looked taller than Traveler remembered, though he was clearly an inch or so shorter than Martin's five feet six. Howe's handshake was fierce, his eye contact riveting, as if he had to prove himself against Traveler's bulk.

His corner office, in shadow except for another mica-shaded desk lamp, seemed as vast as a theater. Traveler knew there had to be both north and west windows, yet there was no sign of light from either of those directions. He and his father followed in Howe's wake like new arrivals to a movie whose eyes haven't yet adjusted to the gloom. As soon as Traveler was seated beside his father in one of two matching client chairs, he closed his eyes to speed up the dilation process.

Howe said, "I hear you're looking for your son."

"It's more complicated than that," Martin answered.

"So I understand from Willis Tanner."

Traveler opened his eyes to see Howe seated across the desk, his elbows planted firmly on a green felt writing pad, his blunt, freckled fingers busily grooming his bushy eyebrows, which matched his close-cropped sandy hair.

"We're here on another matter," Martin said.

"Of course."

"The Chester Building," Traveler put in.

"There's nothing more important than family," Howe said. "Genealogy is a sacred trust. We must track down all who came before us, as well as those who come after. I hope you understand that before it's too late."

Traveler understood all right. He was being warned off the Chester Building, though not in so many words.

"I'm not one for subtlety," Traveler said. "I'd rather have everything out in the open."

"Like me?" a voice said.

A motor whirred. Light began flooding the room from the north. Squinting against the sudden glare, Traveler turned to face the windows whose drapes were being drawn smoothly aside. The figure silhouetted there became recognizable as the apostle Josiah Ellsworth. He was seated in a high-backed chair with exaggerated wings that seemed to enfold him. His hands were clasped around a small leather-bound edition of *The Book of Mormon,* showing a thin gold ribbon as a marker.

Howe stood up as if the shedding of light demanded obeisance from him. With an acknowledging nod, Ellsworth waved him back into his chair.

For Martin's benefit, Traveler introduced the apostle, adding, "He's the one Bill tried to count coup against."

"He did more than try," Ellsworth said. One hand went to his shoulder as if Bill's touch still smarted.

"If it comes to a charge of assault," Howe said, "we have more than enough witnesses to sustain it."

Martin repositioned his chair until he was facing the apostle. Traveler did the same.

Howe continued. "It's my experience that these things are best settled out of court. The fact is—"

Ellsworth silenced Howe with a tapping of the forefinger against the book's leather binding. "As quaint as the Chester Building may be," Ellsworth said, "it's not a landmark. It isn't on the historical register. So why the fuss about saving it? Wouldn't it be better if you gentlemen sought your namesake, another Moroni?"

Out of the corner of his eye, Traveler saw Martin slouch, a sure sign that he was trying to relax away his anger.

Martin said, "Would you prefer a concrete parking structure across the street from the temple?"

"Fresh granite will be quarried from the Wasatch," Ellsworth answered.

"They tell me you're the White Prophet," Martin said.

"Do you believe all the stories you hear?"

"When I was a boy," Martin replied, "they told me the White Prophet was the bogeyman."

"And now?"

"I believe in things a lot worse."

" 'Their torments shall be as a lake of fire and brimstone, whose flame ascendeth up forever and ever.'"

"It's the here and now that worries me." Martin sat up. "When it comes to the Chester Building, are you speaking for Elton Woolley, the prophet?"

Ellsworth looked to Howe who said, "That's Willis Tanner's job. At the moment he's on his honeymoon and can't be reached. If I were you, I'd confine myself to searching out your namesake. Wait too long, and such a search might become impossible."

Martin came out of his chair. "Meaning?"

Ellsworth opened *The Book of Mormon* to the spot marked by the gold ribbon. " 'And thus we see the end of him who perverteth the ways of the Lord; and thus we see that the devil will not support his children at the last day, but doth speedily drag them down to hell.' "

Traveler stepped in front of Martin, blocking his view.

"Is that where you're suggesting we look?" Martin said.

Ellsworth closed the book. "Look to the Lord and to Bingham." He smiled. "Or so we hear."

NINE

Traveler drove while Martin navigated, up South Temple and into Fort Douglas, then along the city's east bench skirting City Cemetery all the way to the State Capitol at the head of State Street. They passed Council Hall, which originally contained the offices of the commander of the Nauvoo Legion, the Mormon army that controlled Utah when it was still a territory. That same Nauvoo Legion had so worried the governor of Illinois that he and his cronies engineered the murder of Joseph Smith in 1844, thereby triggering the Mormon exodus to Utah.

At the end of Traveler's forty-minute drive, no police cars had been visible on a permanent basis, though that was no guarantee they weren't being followed if the FBI-trained church security people were determined enough. Finally, he doubled back as far as the LDS Hospital on Ninth Avenue and D Street, only to find two police cars parked near the emergency entrance and another in the no-parking zone directly out front.

"It probably has nothing to do with Bill," Martin said, "but let's eat first and come back later."

"Steak sandwiches?"

"You read my mind."

The lawn surrounding the Wagon Lunch on Second East looked like it had already died for the winter. It rustled underfoot as Traveler and Martin crossed to the old circus wagon that was sunk hub-deep into the ground. As always, Lou saw them coming and put steaks on his propane grill. Beyond the wagon stood a run-down Hoover bungalow that had been converted into the Wagon Inn.

"I know," Lou said, "extra salt and pepper."

He already had two Grapette sodas standing on the counter. Traveler had been coming there with his father, ordering steak sandwiches with extra salt and pepper and Grapettes, for as long as he could remember. It was one of the places that he and Martin had escaped to when Kary was out for blood.

"Here's another place your mother hated," Martin said as if reading Traveler's mind. "She said I only came here for the beer and had no right bringing you along."

"I seem to remember you having a beer or two."

"I never took you inside the beer joint, did I?"

"Lou kept an eye on me out here."

"You were always hungry, that's why, eating one sandwich after another."

"Those were the days," Lou said. "I made good money then. Look at me now. It's hardly worth the effort firing up my grill for you two." He handed out two paper plates, each with two sandwiches stacked one on top of the other.

They sat on the curb to eat. At the first bite, Traveler sighed. The Wagon Lunch, along with the Snappy Service and Brannings Chili, both over on State Street, were as comforting as the memories they evoked: getaways from Kary, outings after ball games, and dates with good Mormon girls who said no to drinking and smoking but little else.

Martin said, "We only have Claire's word that there is any namesake or that he was put out for adoption."

"Taking money for a kid doesn't qualify as adoption."

"The whole thing could be another of Claire's fantasies, a

way of tormenting us from the grave just the way your mother does."

"If so, maybe Josiah Ellsworth knows it," Traveler said. "Maybe setting us on a wild-goose chase is his way of getting us out of the way."

Martin washed down a mouthful of sandwich with Grapette. "I don't see the Chester Building being important to a man like him, not unless there's something we don't know about."

"I think we can count on that."

Traveler was about to start on his second sandwich when a patrol car rolled to a stop in front of the La Fee Tire Company on the other side of the street. Inside was a single uniformed policeman.

"Who do we have to thank for him?" Martin said. "Anson Horne or Josiah Ellsworth?"

"Who would you rather have for an enemy?"

"We have both, I'm afraid."

Traveler finished his sandwich and returned the empty bottles to Lou. By then, Martin was standing on the sidewalk glaring at the policemen.

"Come on," Traveler said. "We'd better check the hospital before we do anything else."

"I won't be intimidated," Martin said, but allowed himself to be led back to the Ford. "Let's stop by the house on the way. I suddenly feel the need to be armed."

TEN

The house on First Avenue, with adobe walls two feet thick, was a relic from pioneer times, the 1860s, when First Avenue had been known as Fruit Street and the neighborhood as Butcherville because of the nearby slaughter yards. The white picket fence out front hadn't been painted since Traveler's high school days.

The car parked in the driveway didn't have flashing lights on its roof or policemen inside but looked official just the same. Two men young enough to be missionaries got out. Both wore gray suits, white shirts, and narrow, solid brown ties; both had short, military-style haircuts. One was carrying a cellular phone. The other looked from Traveler to the photograph in his hand and nodded to his companion.

"It looks like another call from Willis," Martin said.

"Yes, sir," the one holding the photo said. "We're ready to put you in touch with Mr. Tanner."

"You deal with it, Mo." Martin picked up the day's edition of the *Deseret News* from the doorstep, then went inside and closed the door behind him.

"We've already tested reception. It's fine right here where we are. Our instructions are to connect you and then wait in the car."

The young man with the phone punched in numbers that had been written on the back of the photograph.

"Mr. Tanner, we have Moroni Traveler for you," he said a moment later. "Yes, sir, we're on the front porch at the First Avenue address. No, sir, he's alone. His father's inside. Yes, sir."

They handed the photograph and phone to Traveler and fled to their car.

"If you don't stop causing trouble," Tanner said without preamble, "you're going to ruin my honeymoon. Lael and I have just come now from the temple here in St. George. As the prophet's grandniece, she is disturbed that I have secular duties at a time like this."

"Get to the point, Willis."

"All apostles, numbered and unnumbered, are off limits, Moroni."

"Is that you or the prophet speaking?"

"For once, Mo, take my advice. Stay away from Sam Howe and Josiah Ellsworth. If you persist, I won't be able to help you."

"Bill and Charlie have disappeared," Traveler said.

"I heard that."

"What else have you heard?"

"That Bill committed sacrilege."

"You know better than that. He admires the church more than you think."

"You're the secret admirer, Mo."

"I can't let Bill go to jail for touching someone on the shoulder."

"Be thankful that blood atonement is out of fashion among the Danites."

"Do you know where Bill is?"

"Do you believe in the Danites?" Tanner asked back.

"Are you saying they have Bill and Charlie?"

"Lael sends her love, Mo. She says to tell you she still intends to name our child after you."

"There are too many Moronis as it is."

"She's as stubborn as you are, Mo. I've done my duty by both of you." He hung up.

Traveler left the phone on the porch glider and went inside. Martin was sitting cross-legged in front of the fireplace with half a dozen framed photographs spread on the carpet around him. At Traveler's arrival, he leaned back against the Victorian sofa that had once been Kary's pride and joy and whose velvet upholstery was now covered with sections of the *Deseret News.*

"What do you remember about Gussie Gustavson?" Martin said.

"He owned the Chester Building before Barney, when it was called the Gustavson Building."

Martin nodded before selecting a photograph that showed two young men, Gustavson and Barney Chester, standing in front of the building with their arms around each other's shoulders.

"That was before their falling out," Martin said. "You wouldn't know it to look at Barney now but he was a high-roller in his youth, he and Gustavson both. One night in a high-stakes poker game the building changed hands. It was Gussie's inheritance from his father, along with a salted silver mine and ten thousand shares of worthless penny stock. Witnesses who were there say it was mostly drink combined with natural recklessness that prompted him to offer the building as collateral for his mounting gambling debts. He never thought Barney would actually take possession. Barney might not have, either, if Beau Palmer, his lawyer at the time, hadn't insisted that the bet was legal."

Martin took back the framed photo and handed Traveler another one, a posed group that included Martin and what looked like a very young Nephi Bates.

"Gussie knew the building's history firsthand from his father, who apparently made some kind of deal to get the WPA painters in to do the ceiling. The trouble is, both Gussie and his father are long dead. They did have a collection of photos, though, including shots of the Chester Building through the years. They all went to the State Historical Society."

"Is that where you got these?"

Martin shook his head. "While you were in Park City I scrounged these from Critchlow's office. It's lucky he left them hanging on the walls after he bought the practice from Old Man Palmer."

"I can't see how they help us any."

"Maybe not these, but I put a call in to the Historical Society. Their photographic curator, a man named Wayne Pinock, is out of town for the moment. He's supposed to get back to me in a couple of days. It could be a waste of time, but what the hell. I love looking at the past."

Martin twisted around to grab a section of the *Deseret News* from the sofa behind him. He pointed to a story below the fold where a headline read, KENNECOTT PREDICTS VICTORY IN BINGHAM VOTE.

"The election's only four days away," Martin said. "If Kennecott wins they're going run everybody out of town and start digging up the Oquirrh Mountains. We'd better find young Moroni before that happens."

"The Danites are after Bill and Charlie."

"Is that why Willis called?"

Traveler shrugged. "You know him. It's hard to say for sure."

ELEVEN

The LDS Hospital—once small, church-run, and dedicated to the Saints—had shed its early Prairie style of architecture to become a concrete leviathan. The adjacent square block, once a neighborhood of tall Victorians and Hoover bungalows, had given way to a multilevel concrete parking garage. Traveler left his Fairlane on the main level, partially hidden behind the rusting metal siding meant to screen parked cars from what residents remained in the area. Ten minutes later, he and Martin had tracked down Jubal Hale, the doctor who'd treated Bill. Despite an immaculate white staff coat, fresh dress shirt, and carefully knotted tie, the doctor looked exhausted.

"Your man was one of the easy ones," he said. "He had a clean break. The leg practically set itself. After it was done, though, we had a hard time holding him down until the plaster dried." He shook his head wearily. "We get all kinds in here, of course, but he was the first to have his own Indian medicine man with him, or so the two of them claimed."

Hale rubbed his eyes. "They said they'd come to me seeking enlightenment, not treatment. When I told them I didn't have time to discuss philosophy, they said they'd seek enlightenment elsewhere."

"Where exactly?" Martin asked.

The doctor sighed. "I was about to ask them the same question, figuring I might need some enlightenment myself one day, but they got distracted by Bishop Olsen, one of our regulars who comes here visiting members of his ward whenever anyone's taken ill. The Indian kept tapping the bishop on the shoulder. Every time he did, your friend Bill said, 'Sorry. Only one point per bishop.' You wouldn't happen to know what that's all about, would you?"

Traveler explained the technique of counting coup.

"I envy them their freedom," Hale said. "Anyway, that's the last I saw of them, hustling off down the hall after the bishop, with that friend of yours moving like he'd been born on crutches. I lost sight of them near the nurses' station. You might try there."

At the nurses' station, Traveler got in line behind an elderly man wearing hospital slippers, a flimsy robe, and pushing his own portable stand. A saline drip hung from it feeding into a vein in his left arm.

"Don't mind me," he said, "I'm just getting my exercise and killing time."

With a nod, Traveler stepped around him to talk with the duty nurse. "Dr. Hale sent me. I'm looking for a friend of mine who was treated here for a broken leg."

The woman started shaking her head before Traveler was through speaking. "I have no broken legs in my ward at the moment. You'd better talk to Admitting."

"He's talking about Mr. Williams," the old man said.

"There's no Williams here." The nurse stood up, shook her head again, and walked away.

"Don't mind her," the old man said. "She's overworked like everybody else around here."

"Do you know what happened to Mr. Williams?" Traveler said.

"I was lying down in my room when he and Mr. Redwine

came visiting, along with the bishop." The old man held out a gnarled hand for shaking. "The name's Ezra Gunnison."

"I'm Moroni Traveler. This is my father Martin."

Gunnison clicked his dentures. "He stuck you with a good one, didn't he? Moroni's even worse than Ezra. Ezra Brigham Gunnison. That's what they stuck me with. Come on. They like me to keep moving."

He began shuffling down the hall with Traveler at his side and Martin bringing up the rear.

"They were good company, your Mr. Williams and the Indian. Leastways, they were after they drove off Bishop Olsen. That man gets on my nerves, what with all his reading from the good book. He could put a saint to sleep. You should have seen him clear out; you would have thought Catholics were after him."

"Bill and Charlie, Mr. Williams and Mr. Redwine, have disappeared," Traveler said.

"Frankly, I got the feeling they were hiding in my room, but I didn't care. Time goes slow in this place, so any company is welcome."

"How long did they stay with you?"

"Maybe half an hour. The Indian kept looking out the door. That's why I figured they were hiding out."

Gunnison stopped outside an open door. "This is home. My last one I figure, unless they get tired of me and throw me out." He sighed deeply. "I'm running out of juice and have got to lie down for a while, but you're welcome to come in and sit."

He pushed his drip over to the bed and, with Traveler's help, kept his needle arm safely outside the thin hospital blanket.

"Mr. Redwine told me he was a medicine man and wanted to lay hands on me," Gunnison said. " 'Why not,' I told him, 'everybody else has.' When he let go of me, he said, 'There's no treatment for old age except to make the trip as pleasant as possible.' That's when he offered me a dose of medicine from the bag around his neck. 'They keep me doped to the gills as it is,' I told him, but took a snort just the same. He was right. It made me feel like I could walk right out of here with them.

Mr. Williams wouldn't let me go with him, though. He said he and Charlie had a pilgrimage to do. 'I'm due for one myself,' I told them back, 'when God calls me home.' "

"Did they give a destination?" Martin asked.

" 'Where God lives,' they said, but I figured they were just humoring an old man."

"I'd like to know where he lives myself."

"I've heard said he lives in the temple," Gunnison said, "but I never believed it."

"That's one place I don't think they'll be looking," Martin said.

Gunnison snapped his teeth. "No Gentiles allowed."

"Did you see them leave?" Traveler asked.

"I walked them down the hall, feeling no pain at all, thanks to Mr. Redwine, and saw them out the door. All the time they kept looking around like they couldn't believe their eyes. I guess maybe the cops were after them, because I saw a couple at the admitting desk, but they had their backs turned. I got the impression they didn't give a damn what Mr. Williams or Mr. Redwine did. Hell, maybe I'm imagining things and the police weren't after them at all."

"That's a relief," Martin said. "I was beginning to think they hadn't left under their own steam."

Gunnison sat up in bed. "There were people waiting for them outside, parked right at the curb with the door open."

"Did you see the driver?" Traveler said.

"He got out to meet them, a big guy, not as big as you, though, with one of those short haircuts like we all got in the army."

"Earl Belnap," Martin said.

"It sounds like him," Traveler agreed.

"I never got outside to be introduced," Gunnison said. "I did hear Mr. Williams shout at him, though. 'We're on a pilgrimage,' he hollered. 'You're damn right,' the big guy answered back. He must have been upset because he grabbed Mr. Williams and tried to shove him in the backseat. He hit his head a good one on the roof. I remember saying ouch for him."

Traveler didn't speak again until he and Martin were back in the Fairlane and heading down E Street toward South Temple. "Do you have any idea what's going on?"

"Time was," Martin said, "cops used to drive undesirables out of town and dump them in the desert at the Nevada border, smack in the middle of the salt flats. Of course, they used to beat the shit out of them first. Some say there are a lot of bleached bones still to be found out around Wendover."

"They haven't done that kind of thing for years."

"Gentling the Gentiles, they called it. The tough survived, but they never came back, I can tell you that. But a pair like Bill and Charlie, they could be in real trouble."

"Maybe it wasn't Belnap outside the hospital," Traveler said. "Maybe it was the church."

"Either way, I say we'd better drive out to Wendover and take a look. If nothing else, we can cross over into Nevada and drop a couple of dollars in the slot machines."

TWELVE

Before making the hundred-and-twenty-mile drive across the Great Salt Lake Desert to the Nevada border, Traveler stopped by the office to tell Barney Chester their plans. They found him standing at the cigar counter working on his eternal flame. Freshly oiled pieces of the mechanism were spread on the glass countertop.

"It started to flicker this morning." Chester spoke around the unlit cigar clamped between his teeth. "It must sense the old building's about to die."

He ran a pipe cleaner though a piece of tubing, added it to the other disassembled parts on the counter, then wiped his hands on a rag before setting out three plastic cups and filling them with coffee.

"I've taken it apart twice already," he said. "It still flickers."

"Let me give it a try." Martin began reassembling it while Traveler looked on, sipping coffee.

When Martin had enough pieces together for a test, he struck a match to the spout. The escaping gas made a popping noise before catching fire. The flame burned brightly for a moment, then began sputtering.

"We might as well light up before it dies forever," Chester said. He held out a box of Muriels from his well-stocked counter, which included La Palinas, Robert Burnses, and Upmanns.

Traveler took a cigar to be hospitable, but wouldn't light up while there was work to do, not in Mormon country, where tobacco had been a sin since God gave Joseph Smith the Word of Wisdom. Chester, having no such qualms, began blowing smoke rings toward the ceiling mural.

Martin snuffed out the eternal flame and started disassembling it again. Without looking up from his work, he asked Chester, "What do you know about Gussie Gustavson's photo collection?"

Chester stepped to the end of the counter and spun the rotating postcard rack filled with long-gone sights: the Doll House restaurant, the Black Rock Beach resort, the Coconut Grove, and photographic scenes of Park City when it was still a mining town. The cards, part of Chester's collection, changed occasionally, but were never for sale. Each was protected inside its own clear plastic sleeve.

"Gussie took some of these himself," Chester said. "He was good with a camera. I'll give him that."

"I'm told his son donated the originals to the historical society," Martin said.

"There was a time when Gussie'd stopped drinking and turned to photography. He'd go on snapshot benders and turn up with stacks of photos and drive everyone crazy. You'd see him coming and run. Given half a chance, Gussie would bore you to death with them. I said a prayer of thanksgiving when he went back to the booze."

"Did he take any shots of this building?"

"Like I say, he was snapping all the time when he was sober. Inside, outside, wherever he was. God knows what happened to them all, though I can't see what good they'd do us. If people can't see how beautiful the Chester Building is in person, old snapshots aren't going to change their minds."

"I'm sure you're right," Martin said, "but I want to take a look at them anyway."

Chester blew on the tip of his cigar until it glowed. "If you're going over to the museum, maybe I'll come along with you for a look-see."

"Probably tomorrow," Martin said. "Right now we're driving to Wendover to look for Bill and Charlie."

"What the hell are they doing out there?"

"We don't know where they are for sure," Traveler said, "but my father has a theory."

Martin gave up on the eternal flame and returned the last piece to the countertop. "Most places use rubber hoses. Around here, they gentle the Gentiles."

"Jesus," Barney said. "Are they still doing that?"

"It's a long drive if they aren't," Traveler said.

Martin shrugged. "We can always call Willis and see what he has to say."

"I thought he was on his honeymoon," Chester said.

"He never goes anywhere without a cellular phone, even to bed," Martin said.

Shaking his head, Chester shoved pieces of the eternal flame aside to clear a space on the counter, then carried over his phone and set it on top of the oily glass as if issuing a challenge.

Traveler dialed Willis Tanner's unlisted number. When a machine answered, he entered an access code that Tanner had assigned to him.

"Mr. Tanner is unavailable for the next few days," a recorded voice said. "Please stay on the line if you need further assistance. If you wish another extension, enter that code now."

Traveler waited until a live female voice said, "How may I help you?"

"My name is Moroni Traveler. I'm trying to reach Willis Tanner."

"Could someone else help you?"

"How about Elton Woolley?"

The woman caught her breath as if no one had ever asked to speak to the prophet before.

"Jesus Christ!" Chester said, grabbing for the phone. "Church security is probably tracking the call already."

"Never mind," Traveler told the operator and relinquished his hold on the instrument.

The phone rang as soon as Chester replaced the receiver. He backed away from it immediately.

Traveler started to reach for it, but Martin dragged him away.

"What am I going to do?" Chester called after them.

"Tell them it's a wrong number," Martin answered just before pushing Traveler through the revolving door.

THIRTEEN

Anson Horne's patrol car, if Traveler remembered the license number correctly, was parked in front of the temple gate across the street. He pointed it out to Martin and said, "We'll ask him about gentling the Gentiles."

Since the car was empty, Traveler and Martin entered the temple grounds. The missionaries at the gate said Horne was inside the temple itself, and therefore out of bounds to the likes of Traveler and his father.

"I wonder how they knew we're Gentiles?" Martin said once they were out of earshot of the gatekeepers.

"Can you spot missionaries without being told who they are?"

"I see what you mean."

They sat on the lip of the Sea Gull Monument's reflecting pool where they could keep an eye on the temple, though chances were Horne would be coming from the direction of the annex that connected with the main temple via a ninety-foot tunnel. In either case, Horne couldn't reach the gate without passing by their vantage point.

"How long do we wait?" Martin said.

"Indian summer here in town means the salt flats will be as hot as a frying pan."

"We should have brought lunch and something cold to drink."

Traveler said nothing. They both knew picnicking, like smoking, was strictly prohibited inside the temple grounds.

"Do you think we're procrastinating?" Martin said after a while.

"About the boy, you mean?"

Martin nodded.

"Maybe it's better not to know if Claire was lying to us."

"Maybe it's the responsibility we're afraid of."

Traveler thought that over for a moment. "He won't be ours even if we do find him."

"If I find a grandson, he'll be mine."

"With no blood tie, there's no guarantee of visiting rights."

They talked about child rearing and strategy for hunting down Bill and Charlie until Horne and Sergeant Belnap appeared, heading their way from the direction of the annex.

Traveler and Martin stood up to meet them.

Horne's hair was wet and slicked down; Belnap's crew cut looked matted. Both smelled distinctly of chlorine. Traveler suspected they'd been spending their lunch hour at the baptismal font inside the temple, raising souls. The ritual was accomplished by proxies submerging themselves in the huge cast-iron and porcelain font that stood on the backs of twelve life-size bronze oxen, a design taken from a biblical description of King Solomon's temple. Most likely the policemen had provided relief to the relay teams that conducted continuous baptisms to keep up with the constant demand of raising lost souls to glory. At last count, the church had plans for the raising of a hundred and fifty million.

"I pray for the day when you two will give me an excuse to arrest you," Horne said.

"Amen," Belnap intoned.

"If anyone's broken the law," Martin said, "it's your partner."

Belnap poked a finger in Martin's chest. Traveler reciprocated with a handhold on Belnap's wrist.

"Everybody back off," Horne said. As soon as they had, he glared at Martin. "Let's hear what you have to say."

Traveler watched Belnap's face closely.

Martin said, "Why don't you ask your partner if he's been gentling the Gentiles?"

Belnap's eyes gave him away. Horne must have known too, because he looked away before answering. "That's nothing but an old wives' tale."

"Bullshit," Martin said. "We all know it's the third degree, Mormon style. Bleached bones in the desert along with the leftovers from the Donner party. Only the buzzards do well out there."

Horne turned Belnap around and started him in the direction of the Three Witnesses Monument. "Wait for me there, Earl."

The back of Belnap's neck reddened as he walked away. He stopped a few feet from the monument to stare at the gray granite block covered with bas-relief depictions of David Whitmer, Oliver Cowdery, and Martin Harris, the men who testified that the Angel Moroni had shown them the golden tablets that revealed *The Book of Mormon* to Joseph Smith. From a distance, Belnap's hunched shoulders made it look as if he were denying any such revelation.

"I'll have a talk with Earl," Horne said.

"If anything's happened to Bill and Charlie," Traveler said, "I'll be coming for him. You tell him that."

Horne stared at Traveler, narrowing his eyes as if trying to assess the threat. Finally, he nodded. "Let's say Earl did it—and I'm not admitting anything—well, he's no fool. He wouldn't risk killing them. He'd be careful to dump them within walking distance of Wendover."

FOURTEEN

Going west from Salt Lake City, I-80 climbs out of Skull Valley into the seven-thousand-foot Cedar Mountains. Once beyond them, the highway descends gradually into that great four-thousand-square-mile sinkhole known as the Salt Lake Desert, the bed of prehistoric Lake Bonneville. Even on maps, it was portrayed as white, the color of salt; it supported no life of any kind.

Traveler lowered his sun visor, which failed to dispel the shimmering water mirage into which the highway seemed to disappear. Above the water, a phantom mountain range glided across the horizon as indolently as a Gila monster.

Eighty miles out from the city, he shook his head hard to make certain that Knolls, the old Western Pacific Railroad siding, was real. Beyond Knolls, I-80 didn't so much as curve again for forty miles.

To keep awake, he switched on the Cherokee's radio, which Martin kept tuned to KBYU, the church's university station, which played classical music. This far from town, its signal was overridden by country and western booming somewhere out of Nevada.

"Find something else," Traveler said. "I'm having trouble keeping my eyes open"

"All you have to do is close them," Martin answered, "and you can see the Donner party. Out there in the desert, their wagons sunk to the hubs in the crusted sand, struggling, spending themselves even before they reached the Sierras. Nowadays our military would put those pilgrims out of their misery here and now."

He was referring, Traveler knew, to the vast Hill Air Force Bombing Range that lay to the north of them; to the south was the Dugway Proving Grounds, where the army tested the nastiest of its chemical weapons, often as not on the livestock of nearby ranchers.

Martin fiddled with the radio but the only strong signals belonged to rock-and-roll and country-music stations.

"Your choice," Martin said.

"Talk to me."

Martin turned off the radio and said, "Do you remember the I & M outings?"

"One of them. I was seven or eight, I think. I remember playing softball, eating hot dogs, and drinking sodas, but mostly it rained."

"That was my last company picnic, up in the Heber Valley, behind Mount Timpanogos. Shortly after that, I left the I & M and took up police work. That decision changed my life. Yours too."

The I & M Rug and Linoleum Company on South State Street had been a magical place to Traveler as a boy. Its vast warehouse filled with carpet rolls, furniture frames waiting to be upholstered, lines of sofas, and unopened cardboard cartons stacked ceiling-high was the perfect place for games of hide-and-seek on those days when Kary dropped him off. *I have shopping to do,* she'd say. *Stay out of the way. Don't cause trouble.* What she really wanted, Traveler had sensed even then, was to be rid of him for a while. *Your father won't be long,* she'd say. But sometimes she dropped him off right after lunch, which meant a five-hour wait until closing, a long time to play hide-and-seek without a seeker.

"Do you remember why I left the I & M?" Martin asked.

"To better yourself."

"That was your mother talking. That's what she insisted I tell you at the time. It was one of those periods when your mother and I weren't living together."

"You were a carpet layer at the I & M," Traveler said.

"That's what Kary called it. Actually, I was on my way to being shop foreman. With profit sharing, it would have paid a lot more than the police department."

"If you hadn't been a cop, there'd be no Moroni Traveler and Son."

"Your mother hated that worse than carpet laying."

"You didn't last long as a policeman."

"Your mother kept after me to go into business for myself. I owe her for that. For you, too."

Traveler concentrated on the road ahead, running through conversations with his mother. *Your father has no ambition. If you're not careful, you'll end up just like him. Don't come crying to me when that happens. I want people to look up to my son. I want him to be someone.*

"Why did you move out that time?" Traveler said.

"Knowing your mother, you shouldn't have to ask."

"Another man?"

Martin snorted. "That woke you up, didn't it." He bent over the radio again, tuning up and down the dial until he found a weak-signaled news station.

Traveler was still wide-awake thirty minutes later when they reached the city of Wendover sprawled across the Utah-Nevada border. Originally founded as a watering hole for the Western Pacific, Wendover became an oasis for motorists in 1925 when the first highway was completed. During World War II, twenty thousand people were moved there to service a gigantic air force base that eventually trained the atomic-bomb pilots. Wendover's present-day population had subsided to a thousand or so.

"Where do we start looking?" Martin said.

"That's as good a place as any." Traveler indicated the Hard Times Redemption Center, the first pawn shop on the Utah side, where Kary had once sold Martin's car to pay for one of her sprees to the Coast.

"Redemption," Martin muttered. "Bill and Charlie would like the sound of that."

The pawnbroker remembered the pair immediately. "They weren't your usual gamblers," he said. "I could see that right off. In the first place, they weren't dressed well enough. They sure as hell didn't look like they had anything worth pawning. They fooled me, though. That's what I love about this business, the people you meet. Where else would you run into an Indian and a guy on crutches claiming to be God's prophet?"

The pawnbroker held up a Navajo amulet. "The Indian was wearing this under his shirt, along with a medicine bag. I get softhearted once in a while so I gave them ten bucks' eating money for both items."

"What was in the bag?" Martin said.

"Empty, I'm afraid." The man winked. "I would have paid more otherwise."

"I'll redeem them," Traveler said.

"You don't have a receipt."

"Those are sacred relics."

"I've heard that before."

"Here's my card. You can come after me if there's any trouble."

"I'm trusting you," the pawnbroker said, "along with a redemption bonus, of course."

Once Traveler had the medicine bag and amulet, he said, "Do you know where they went from here?"

"The last I saw, they were like everyone else I meet, heading in the direction of the nearest casino." He went to the window and pointed toward the State Line.

The State Line Casino straddled Utah and Nevada, with a painted white line running down the middle of the floor to mark the demarcation. On the Utah side only 3.2 beer was legal; on the Nevada side, everything that money could buy was available.

The security man at the door, a two-hundred-pounder trying unsuccessfully to look like a patron instead of a bouncer, pointed a finger at Martin. "The gun stays outside, old-timer."

Most times Martin would have bristled at being called old, but at the moment information came first.

"I must be getting past it," Martin said with a self-condemning shake of his head. "I forgot all about the damned thing."

While he went to lock the .45 in the Jeep, Traveler handed the bouncer a twenty. "We're looking for some friends of ours. A tall man, my height, pear-shaped around the waist, walking on crutches. He has an Indian with him."

"If you're going to drop the hammer on them, pal, don't do it around here."

Traveler surrendered a business card along with another twenty.

The bouncer nodded before tucking away the offerings. "They didn't have any luck at all. The slots wiped them out in two minutes. When they started panhandling, I had to escort them on their way."

"Gently, I hope."

"They didn't cause me any trouble, if that's what you mean, though the Indian did say something weird, something about recharging his medicine in the desert."

Martin returned, pulling up his shirttails to show he was unarmed.

"Take it from me," the bouncer said after giving him the once-over, "the management here doesn't want word getting around that they're taking the sucker's prescription money. So

I says to the Indian, 'If you're feeling sick, maybe I can get you something.' The Indian doesn't say a word to that, just folds his arms and stares at me. That's when the other one, the guy with the cast on his hoof, asks for directions to the nearest Indian settlement. 'I'll be damned,' I says to myself, but I'm a Good Samaritan. So I dug a road map out of my car and came up with the Skull Valley Indian Reservation."

Martin groaned. "That's a hundred miles back the way we came."

"I told them the same thing. You know what the big guy said to that? 'God will show us the way. His desert will purify us.' I've heard a lot of hard-luck stories, I can tell you that, but nothing that crazy. For a minute there, I figured it was just talk, what with him claiming to be a prophet. Besides, I make it a rule never to get involved with the customers, though sometimes their sad faces can eat you alive. But this time I said to myself, 'You don't want these two on your conscience.' So I sprung for some bottled water before sending them on their way.

"I stood right outside the door and watched them head for the highway. And you know what? The big guy was right. God did provide. They hadn't gone three hundred yards up the highway before an old pickup truck stopped to give them a ride. Considering the way those two looked, it was a miracle. I sure as hell wouldn't have picked up hitchhikers like that, but Bob Campbell's softhearted. At least, I think that's who was driving. It looked like his truck anyway. Bob's got a place out on the Dugway road, halfway to the reservation. Sort of a rest stop for tourists, with live rattlesnakes and things like that. An oasis, he calls it."

FIFTEEN

Traveler gassed the Jeep and checked the radiator before heading back toward Salt Lake. During the drive, they kept a constant watch on either side of the highway for any sign of Bill and Charlie. When they reached the railroad siding at Knolls, Traveler pulled off the road and stopped. "Why would Charlie head for Skull Valley? That's a Goshute reservation, not Navajo. They wouldn't have him even if he did show up and ask for asylum."

"So where does that leave us?"

Traveler spread the auto-club map across the dashboard, which was hot to the touch in the ninety-degree sun. "Here's where the Dugway road turns off at Rowley Junction." He pointed to a spot thirty miles ahead of them on I-80, then ran his finger along the base of the Stansbury Mountains, past the Skull Valley Indian Reservation, and into the town of Dugway, a distance of about seventy miles from their present location. He backtracked to point out the only intermediate stop, an old ghost town named Iosepa.

"I remember that place," Martin said. "The church settled

Hawaiian converts there in the 1880s. The desert did its best to kill them, but it was leprosy that got them in the end. Even Bill isn't goofy enough to head for there."

Martin thumped his forehead with the palm of his hand. "I remember now. There was a roadhouse on the Dugway road we used to go to just after the war. In those days, it was considered the thing to do, drive out in the dark, get drunk, and drive back like maniacs. I think it was called the Last Stop Oasis. It must be the place the bouncer told us about."

The Last Stop Oasis, built to look like an oversize log cabin, was now called Bob's Big Indian. Gaps showed in the chinking between the logs, and the leaning rock chimney was braced by weathered two-by-fours. Two fake tepees, decorated with faded buffalos, stood out front in the dusty gravel parking area, along with a battered pickup truck. Charlie sat cross-legged in front of one tepee door slit, Bill the other. Both were stripped to the waist and covered with war paint, which Charlie had once claimed to be the perfect sunscreen. Both pounded on drums, keeping the beat as Traveler and Martin marched toward them. Both sat on thick books to protect themselves from the sun-scorched gravel, which Traveler distinctly felt through the soles of his shoes.

"You talk to them," Martin said. "I'm going inside for a cold beer."

As Traveler squatted, Bill reached into the tepee behind him, brought out another book, and handed it over. *The History of Utah Art* felt cool to the touch. Traveler slid it under him and sat down.

"Books have many uses," Charlie said.

Traveler, half blinded by the sunlight bouncing off the gravel, couldn't read the Indian's expression. "What the hell are you two doing out here?"

"God sent us into the desert to burn away our sins and seek truth through visions," Bill said. "Like he does with all his prophets."

"The police dumped you at the border."

"God has his own ways."

"We came to take you home."

Bill shook his head. "We've been sent here to help Bob in his time of need. We are his main attraction."

Traveler shifted to a crouch in order to retrieve his book. When he turned it over he saw a sale sticker with a price of $25. "That's a bit expensive, isn't it?"

Bill shrugged. "Bob set up business here to bring enlightenment to tourists and locals alike."

"And he provides the books?"

"God provides them."

"A man from the church brought them to us," Charlie said.

"He was God's messenger," Bill clarified. "Bob only priced them."

"Who are you talking about?" Traveler said.

"It's never wise to question God or his messengers."

Traveler looked around the parking lot, empty except for Martin's Jeep and the pickup that had BOB'S BIG INDIAN stenciled on the door.

"Tourists come here to take our pictures sometimes," Charlie said.

"Bob used to be a writer," Bill went on. "He gave it up to act as a Good Samaritan to people crossing the desert. If he'd been here when the Donner party came through, who knows how many lives would have been saved. He tells us he dreams about them every night."

Charlie gripped the new medicine bag that hung around his neck, a cloth one that looked as if it had once contained marbles. It also looked empty. "We all dream," the Indian said.

Bill laid a hand on the gravel. "Feel the heat, Moroni. Feel God's cleansing power."

With a creaking of knee cartilage, Traveler rose to his feet. "You must have sunstroke. Now come on. I've got work to do back in the city."

Bill reached into the tepee again and retrieved another book, a thinner, paperbound volume entitled *Utah's Historic Archi-*

tecture. "We have our own work here, Moroni. You would be wise to join us."

"It's a long walk back to the Chester Building."

"God will show us the way," Bill said.

"When you run out of faith," Traveler said, "phone us and we'll come get you." He leaned over and dropped the amulet and leather medicine pouch in Charlie's lap.

"You see how God provides," Bill observed. "Donations to our church, the Church of the True Prophet."

Charlie turned over his drum, revealing a hollow side, which he held out toward Traveler.

"I'll be in Bingham for a day or two." Traveler dropped in two twenties. "If you can't reach me or Martin, leave a message with Barney."

SIXTEEN

Martin insisted on fixing a big breakfast the next morning, stacking hotcakes four-high on Traveler's plate and surrounding them with strips of crisp bacon. The maple syrup was hot, with the butter melted right into it.

The smell took Traveler back to leisurely Sunday mornings when Kary was still alive, though the taste reminded him that Martin had always been the cook in the family.

"I want you at your best when you go looking for my grandson," Martin announced. "I also want you to watch yourself out there in Bingham."

His tone of voice made elaboration unnecessary. They both knew that Bingham was a rough, company-dominated mining town and had been that way for more than a hundred years. Over that time it had been settled in waves by Serbs, Croatians, Mexicans, Italians, Greeks, Japanese, French, Germans, all of whom fought constantly with one another, but would be certain to close ranks against an outsider like Traveler.

"Come to think of it," Martin added, "maybe I'd better come with you."

"One stranger in town will be bad enough. Two would be impossible. On top of that, you've got the Chester Building to worry about."

"This may be the only chance I get at a grandson."

"All I'm going to do is look around, not steal him for you."

"The least you can do is bring me back a snapshot of the boy," Martin said.

"I don't want to be too conspicuous."

"I've been thinking about that. It might be best if you called yourself Martin like I do. There's no use calling attention to the similarity in the first names. One Moroni Traveler looking for another would be sure to raise eyebrows."

"You're assuming that Claire's story was true, that she gave him up only on condition that his name never be changed."

"The Traveler part must have been dropped by now. But why take chances? Call yourself Martin and be done with it. I've found it helpful over the years, even soothing at times." He pushed his half-eaten hotcakes aside. "You'd better take my Jeep, too. I don't think your old Ford will make it on those mountain roads."

Traveler accepted the car keys. "I should be back for dinner. If something comes up, I'll call and let you know."

"Just keep Kennecott in mind. Their damned election is only three days away."

"If the boy's there, I'll find him."

"Maybe I'll get a sign painter while you're gone. I'll have him add an S to 'Moroni Traveler and Son.' "

Fifteen minutes later, with the pancakes lumped in his stomach, Traveler picked up the old Bingham highway and headed southwest toward the Oquirrh Mountains twenty-five miles away. Because they were the first mountains in the Great Salt Lake Basin to reflect the sunrise, the Paiute Indians called them the shining mountains, the Oquirrhs. They were said to be the richest ore-bearing range on the continent.

They were blue-gray at the moment, with smoke from the

smelters hanging motionless in their ravines. As the highway rose, climbing out of old Lake Bonneville, it entered the small canyon town of Copperton, which hadn't changed since the 1930s when the Utah Copper Company, now Kennecott, built it as a company town.

Beyond Copperton, near the ghost town of Lead Mine, late-summer rains had nurtured a second crop of yellow sunflowers and lavender skunkweed on the hillsides, along with straggly thickets of elderberries and chokecherries.

After Lead Mine, the road wound its way through Dry Fork, past the abandoned remains of the English Dairy, and across Damphaol Gulch. At that point a dirt track, known as Damn Fool Road, branched to the left. Traveler resisted the temptation to follow it and continued ahead until the two-lane asphalt narrowed before entering the short tunnel that led to the town of Bingham Canyon itself. He checked the rearview mirror, saw no traffic, and stopped in the middle of the road. He hadn't seen another car since leaving the floor of the basin.

With the engine running, he got out to study the deep, narrow canyon that had once been home to red pine, maple, and oak. Now there was nothing but scrub, and in places even that had been burned away by old mine tailings that had spilled down the steep banks like blood from a wound.

Traveler hadn't been in Bingham since the night of his high school graduation, when he and some friends had been attracted by the town's reputation—saloons where no one asked for IDs and a notorious red-light district unthinkable anywhere else in Utah. Four of them had made the drive that night: Traveler, Walt Kilbourn, Gordy Christensen, and Willis Tanner; they all talked big on the first part of the drive, but grew quiet the closer they got to the town. That night, too, they'd stopped just short of Bingham's landmark tunnel because Walt, their driver, got cold feet.

"Dad'll kill me," he'd said, "if we get picked up in his car."

"Stay sober, then," Willis said. "Play old maid while we raise a little hell."

"We could just drive around and take a look, then go back to town for something to eat."

"We came here to celebrate," Tanner said. "Who knows when we'll get another chance like this."

"We could get into trouble."

"Nobody gives a damn out here in Bingham." Tanner smacked his lips. "They say the whores are something. I've got the address memorized—520 Main Street."

"We could get a disease."

"You brought rubbers, didn't you?"

"I forgot." Walt sounded relieved.

"Relax. I've got plenty to go around." Tanner handed out sealed packs to everyone.

"We could get rolled," Walt pleaded.

"He's got a point," Gordy chimed in.

"So we'll all stick close to Moroni. Nobody's going to pick on someone his size."

"Is that why you brought me along?"

Willis had grinned then. "Just do as I do, Moroni."

Traveler smiled at the memory and drove into the tunnel. On the other side, the road became Main Street and was barely wide enough for two cars to pass. It would stay that way, running along the bottom of the steep V-shaped canyon, as it ascended toward Kennecott Copper's enormous, ever-expanding open-pit mine. Every so often, gulches crisscrossed Main Street, each leading to ancillary mining camps: Carr Fork, Highland Boy, Lark, Copperfield, Dinkeyville, Jap Camp, and Frogtown. There were no trees, no flowers either, nothing but blackened hillsides and blackening buildings.

Traveler bypassed Frogtown's Amicone Bar, Christ Apostles Grocery, and the Liberty Bell Bakery, and continued on up Main Street, intending to begin his quest in the center of Bingham Canyon, at the crossroads known as the Bingham Mercantile Corner, Bingham Merc for short.

Along the way, most places were closed, either by the Kennecott buyout or hard times. The old Yampa Smelter had outlived its usefulness, as had the Bourgard Slaughterhouse, though it had left a lingering smell behind.

So steep was the canyon, that miners' shacks, boarding-houses, and businesses alike had been squeezed up against the narrow roadway. Sidewalks were afterthoughts and backyards were forty-five-degree slopes. In places, the canyon wall had been gouged out to accommodate a second row of shacks, squeezed so close that one man's roof became another's front porch.

At a point where the canyon widened slightly, Traveler parked in front of city hall, a two-story brick building across from the Bingham Merc. The slaughterhouse smell had given way to a metallic taste in his mouth, as if he'd been sucking on a penny. He swallowed grimly and climbed the stone steps that matched the building's dingy windowsills and cornices.

He half expected to find the door locked. When it opened he felt compelled to knock and call out, "Is anyone here?"

"I'll be right with you," a woman answered from deeper inside the building.

He waited in the hallway, next to a scarred wooden desk, a teacher's model old enough to have a disappearing typewriter well. A stack of newspapers, the *Bingham Bulletin*, lay on the desktop. A map of Bingham Canyon, a good ten feet long, with crease marks indicating that it had originally been some kind of fold-out, was taped to the plaster wall behind the desk. Traveler was trying to locate himself on it when a door across the hall opened and a woman said, "I hope you're not another reporter here about the election?"

He was tempted to lie. Newsmen were more palatable to most people than private detectives, even one on a personal mission. But when he looked at her, a thin, bony woman wearing wire-rimmed glasses and a severe look that reminded him of his English teacher, Miss Tregagle, all he could say was, "No, ma'am."

"Reporters have been coming and going around here for the last week, pestering everybody in town," she said. "Every time you say anything to them, they change your words, put them in the paper, and stir up trouble."

She gave him a once-over worthy of Miss Tregagle. "Thanks to all the publicity, our volunteer help has dried up. The mayor has had to go into hiding to get any work done. Not that I blame people for taking precautions, or taking inventory of their belongings in case we all have to move out. In any case, young man, I don't know who it is you want to see, but you're going to have to settle for me. I'm Ida Odegaard and I'm the only one here."

"My name's Martin," he said.

She raised an eyebrow before tucking a stray hair back into place.

"I'm looking for someone," he went on, "and thought I'd better do it before the election."

"You may have missed them already. Kennecott's been at it for years, buying up properties and tearing them down. Most of my friends are long gone, sold out or evicted. In its heyday, Bingham Canyon had nearly three thousand souls. Now I figure we're only a tenth of that. It makes you want to cry sometimes, seeing places you love close down one after the other. My husband's family, the Odegaards, are third generation, though some old-timers around here can trace their families all the way back to the beginning, when Brigham Young sent settlers into the Oquirrhs to farm and cut timber. He didn't know the half of it, though, did he? That his people were sitting on a fortune out here, on mountains of copper. They say our town is standing on top of ten million tons of ore."

Traveler nodded to keep her talking.

"The joke is," she said, nodding back, "old Brigham didn't believe in mining. A man's duty was to till the land and raise a family, not to get rich quick. Now Kennecott says it has to expand the mine or die. If you ask me, we need another Brigham Young to stand up against the company."

She stared at Traveler as if measuring his chances against such an opponent. "You never did say who it is you're looking for."

"The Tempest family," he said.

"In the old days, the company used paid informers to ferret out troublemakers. Some say they still have spies, though these days union men don't get beaten to death or disappear. They just get leaned on until they sell out. A man your size could do a lot of damage if he leaned on somebody."

"I don't work for Kennecott, if that's what you're asking. I'm looking for a lost relative and was told the Tempests might be able to help me."

She rose up on tiptoe to look him in the eye. What she saw made her purse her lips. "Leaving reporters out of it, you're not the first to come around here snooping, what with my husband's leading the opposition against Kennecott. Are you for or against selling out to the company?"

"It's not my fight."

She stared at him so hard the loose flesh beneath her eyes quivered.

"Maybe I'd better try the newspaper office," he said.

She pointed to the stack of *Bulletins* on the desk. "That's the last issue you're likely to see. Even if we win the election, there isn't enough of us left to make this town a worthwhile proposition."

He thanked her and started for the door.

"I heard the Tempests were renting a place up in Copperfield," she called after him.

He hesitated at the threshold.

"To get there you go through the long tunnel."

"Do you have an address?" he asked.

"Come to think of it, Kennecott has closed down most of Copperfield already. They were just powder-box cabins anyway. The best you can do is ask around when you get there. With the town shrinking the way it is, just about anybody ought to be able to tell you where to find the Tempests."

Mrs. Odegaard could, too, he thought, if she had the inclination. Sending him to Copperfield was probably a ruse so she could alert the Tempests. If that was true, his search could be over quickly, or develop complications.

"Is there someplace in town I could stay overnight?" he asked, in case the search took him longer than expected.

"We used to have some fine places in the canyon, the Seminole Hotel up in Carr Fork, and the Belmont. They're both gone now, so's the Elmerton down near the mouth of Markham Gulch. We had some good boardinghouses, too, in the old days."

"And now?"

"You take my advice and try Emma Dugan's place. It used to be a boardinghouse, when there were any boarders. She's all but closed up now. You tell her I sent you and she'll open up a room for you."

Traveler must have looked skeptical, because she added, "There's no place else, young man, not safe anyway. Stay away from the blind pigs. But you do what you want. You look like the kind who would anyway."

"Where do I find Emma Dugan?"

"You keep going up Main Street. When you see the old Bingham Mortuary, that's the ground floor of the Bourgard Apartments, you'll know you've gone half a block too far."

"Is there a bishop in town I could talk to?"

She smiled for the first time. "There never were that many Mormons in the canyon, though we did have a ward house once. These days there aren't enough of the Saints left to make it worthwhile. The fact is, none of our churches will be open much longer. It's a shame. We don't even have services on a regular basis. Old Papa Joe is still around, though. He's a retired priest, an Orthodox Croat, who was born here and whose father was a miner before him. You can usually find him at the Bingham Merc, telling tales and talking about the good old days. What he's going to do if we sell out to Kennecott, I don't know. Our other priest, Father Bannon, I'd stay away from."

SEVENTEEN

Once outside city hall, Traveler hesitated. Although conscious that Mrs. Odegaard was still watching him, he made no move to cross the street to the Bingham Merc, where Papa Joe could be found. Once he started asking questions nothing would be the same again, not for him, not for Martin, and probably not the boy. If he walked away now, chances were Ida Odegaard might not even tell the Tempests about him. Even if she did, they wouldn't know where to find him, and probably wouldn't want to.

And what the hell was he going to say to the Tempest family anyway? I'm here about my son, who isn't really mine, but who's named after me. The son Claire Bennion sold to you.

If indeed there had been a sale, the Tempests were party to a crime. Then again, maybe no money changed hands, maybe there wasn't a child either, just another of Claire's games. In that case, nothing would be lost but Traveler's pride.

He shook his head. Pride had nothing to do with it. The boy came first. Assuming his existence, the Tempests would be the only family he'd ever known. To disturb that relationship would only compound Claire's madness.

Martin's parting words, shouted as Traveler was pulling out of the driveway, echoed inside Traveler's head. *Don't forget. I want a snapshot of my grandson.*

I'll make sure he's happy and well taken care of, Traveler answered now, *but only if I can manage it without causing trouble.*

To give himself more time to think, he decided to forgo interviewing the priest or looking for a room and walk to Copperfield. When he reached the narrow, single-lane tunnel leading to Copperfield, the signal light was green, meaning traffic was free to pass through the underpass from this side. Signs posted on the tunnel facing said, PEDESTRIANS NOT AL-LOWED ON ROADWAY, MUST USE SIDEWALK, and ONE-WAY TRAF-FIC, DRIVERS MUST OBEY LIGHT SIGNALS. Also posted was a twenty-mile-an-hour speed limit by order of S. Grant Young, Sheriff.

The arched tunnel mouth itself was just a hole in the mountain surrounded by concrete, ugly and utilitarian, like a patch slapped against the soil to keep it in check. As soon as Traveler stepped into the opening, with seven thousand feet of narrow pedestrian walkway stretching ahead of him, he began moving quickly. There were no sound except for that of his own footsteps.

Looking for the Tempests was one thing, he told himself; asking questions about them to determine their suitability as parents quite another. Any kind of in-depth background check would be sure to trigger small-town gossip. The best approach, then, was a direct confrontation once he located the family.

When he emerged from the tunnel fifteen minutes later, the day seemed much hotter. Ninety degrees at least, he guessed, hot enough for heat waves to make the shanties seem to hover precariously on the hillside. No more than half a dozen cars were parked on the street. The only sign of life was an old dog sunning itself in front of an abandoned house. The animal's tail wagged once at Traveler's passing.

The Rex Hotel, its weather-blackened clapboard siding on the verge of disintegration, was boarded up, as was the Copperfield Theater. Dirty plywood had been nailed over the windows of the Lendaris Market. The Miner's Merc was nothing but a shell. As far as Traveler could see, Copperfield was a ghost town in the making.

He was about to turn back when he saw movement out of the corner of his eye. Until that moment, the two men sitting on the shaded porch of the U.S. Hotel had been as still as wooden Indians. Setting their rockers in motion, he felt certain, had been a deliberate way of attracting his attention.

Traveler joined them, sitting on the lip of the porch to make himself less threatening, though judging from the winks they exchanged he needn't have bothered. Another city slicker, their expressions said, to be dealt with and sent on his way.

Both men had deeply wrinkled, sun-scorched faces; both looked to be in their seventies; both wore bib overalls, grimy-looking flannel shirts, and hightop boots. Their baseball caps set them apart, one a blue Los Angeles Dodger, the other a Cincinnati Red.

"If you're looking for a story," the Dodger fan said, "we started charging a long time ago. Stories about the old days, that's what they all want to hear. Stories about the strike and the company thugs."

"I was looking to get out of the sun," Traveler said.

"They say it causes cancer."

"I've heard that."

"They ought to try breathing in the mines," the Dodger said.

His companion adjusted his red cap. "He's right, young man. You spend time underground and you learn to appreciate the sun. It's open-pit mining now, of course, but not when we started out. Then you tunneled like a goddamn gopher."

"I'm not a reporter," Traveler said.

The two exchanged confirming nods.

"We didn't think you were," the Cincinnati man said, "but it will still cost you."

"How much?"

"On a hot day like this, there's nothing like an ice-cold soda."

Traveler took out a twenty-dollar bill and handed it over.

"Joe boy," they both called together. "Come out here."

A young boy appeared from around the side of the ramshackle hotel. Traveler guessed his age at about ten, though his fancy sneakers looked big enough for a teenager.

"If you give Joe boy here three dollars," Cincinnati said, "he'll run home and get us some colas."

Traveler eyed the pocket into which the twenty had disappeared, then counted four singles into the boy's outstretched hand. "Get one for yourself, too, Joe."

The boy ran off, raising dust and attracting the dog from down the block. Both disappeared into a narrow alley.

"Kids are like dogs," the Dodger said. "They grow into their feet." He pointed at Traveler. "I'm betting Joe boy will be as big as you are someday, Mr. . . ."

"Martin," Traveler said.

"Well, Mr. Martin, you look like a company man to us." He stamped his foot on the porch's warped wooden slats. "The fact is, this used to be a company boardinghouse. They'd pay you spit for digging their copper, then take it away from you for living here. What they didn't get went to the girls down at 520 Main." He smiled at the memory. "They were worth every damn penny of it, though."

"I wish they were back in business," his cohort said. "I'd go down there and die happy." He touched the bill of his red cap like a base coach sending signals.

The Dodger acknowledged by tipping his head. "Now what is it we can do for you?"

"How many people are still living here in Copperfield?" Traveler said.

"Maybe a dozen."

"Not that many," his friend said. "There's no reason to stay. The electricity's still on, but the phones are long gone."

"They say the company's cutting off the electricity next week," the Dodger said.

The boy returned at a dead run, the dog trotting beside him, tongue lolling. The cans of cola were well shaken by the time he handed them out. The boy immediately stepped back, out of splash range.

Traveler angled his can at the road and pulled the tab, sending a spray of soda halfway across the narrow street.

"How many times have we told you not to run with the sodas?" the Dodger said.

The boy shrugged and disappeared around the side of the Rex, shaking his cola can as he went. The dog stared after him for a moment, then went back to where it had come from, lying in the sun down the block.

Both men set their sodas aside and stared at Traveler while he drank what was left of his.

"Your twenty's running out of time," the Cincinnati man said finally.

"I'm looking for the Tempest family," Traveler admitted.

"Everybody but fools like us have moved back down to Bingham, though how long they'll be staying on there is anybody's guess.

"Are you saying the Tempests moved down the canyon?" Traveler said.

"Who said they ever lived up here?"

Traveler shrugged. "Do you know where I can find them?"

The Dodger fingered the bill of his cap, while the Cincinnati Red removed his and wiped its stained sweatband.

"These days," Cincinnati said, "I don't know where to find anybody but myself. After the election, God knows where we'll end up, probably lost in some old-folks' home down in the valley."

"It's a hell of a thing," the Dodger added, "old miners like us having to relocate to la-di-da places like Magna or Bacchus."

Both men spit to show their disgust at such a prospect.

"What about the Tempests?" Traveler said again.

"Keep asking," Cincinnati said. "You never know. Someone might take pity on you."

Traveler resisted the temptation to ask for his twenty back, thanked them, and started back toward the tunnel. By the time he reached the mouth, he glanced back to see the boy, Joe, following him.

When Traveler emerged from the tunnel, the boy had closed the gap between them until he was only a few yards behind.

"You can come up here and walk with me," Traveler called over his shoulder, but the boy shook his head.

Traveler walked slowly, looking for someone to talk to. But everything was closed, abandoned judging by their looks: Wells Grocery, Cho Cho's Chocolate Shop, Bingham Meat, Berg's Furniture, the Utah Copper Hospital. Even the *Bingham Bulletin* had a sign on the door saying, CLOSED FOR THE DURATION.

The Rexall Drugs looked abandoned, so did Royal Candy Number 1, the Gem Theater, and Bert Thaxton's barber shop. The brothel at 520 Main was boarded up. Only the Copper Keepsake showed signs of life, with a window full of metal-plated souvenirs, arrowheads, miniature tea sets, and picture postcards with shiny copper nuggets pasted to them. He tried the door, found it locked, and wondered how long the BACK IN FIFTEEN MINUTES sign had been hanging in the window.

With a sigh, Traveler stepped off the sidewalk to get a better look at 520 Main. The second-floor windows, as murky now as sightless eyes, had been filled with light on graduation night, with waving girls perched on every sill, shouting down encouragement.

"The one on the end's for me," Willis Tanner had said.

Even from a distance she looked old enough to be his mother, or Traveler's mother, which made her all the more exciting.

"How much?" Tanner called to her.

"I give a discount to virgins," she answered back. "Just ask for Angel Mary."

"You're going to lose money on these two, then," Tanner said, pushing Walt Kilbourn and Gordy Christensen ahead of him toward the door.

A force field of perfume surrounded the madam who greeted them. She was a middle-aged, bone-thin woman with bright hennaed hair and a low-cut gown to match. Blue veins showed beneath the milky skin of her corseted, upthrust breasts. Her welcoming smile killed Traveler's hope that they'd be thrown out because of their age.

"We have a parade every fifteen minutes," she said. "You pay your money and take your choice."

"Angel Mary," Willis said.

The madam winked and sang out:

> "Angel Mary heist your leg,
> Take that Mormon down a peg,
> While I roll your sister Meg,
> Upon the parlor floor."

The tune went with ditties Traveler had heard his father sing.

"You pay me, honey," she said, "but if you tip Angel Mary enough, she'll show you the wonders of the world."

Tanner paid.

"What about the rest of you?" the woman said once she'd tucked away the money.

Christensen and Kilbourn fled, but Tanner had Traveler by the arm.

"He's bashful," Tanner said.

Her eyes changed momentarily, showing something almost motherly. "Come on," she had said, taking Traveler's hand while signaling another woman to take over door duty, "I'll show you the wonders myself."

Traveler turned away from 520 Main, away from the memory of that sad woman, to ask the boy, "Is the Copper Keepsake still in business?"

The boy nodded. Traveler looked up and down the street, saw no sign of a shopkeeper, and decided to head for the Bingham Merc rather than wait.

EIGHTEEN

All eyes turned toward Traveler when he entered the Bingham Mercantile. The tall man wearing a black Eastern Orthodox robe paused in midgesture, one hand raised above his gray head as if pointing toward heaven. His audience of two, miners obviously, with grit ground into their hands and arms, stared at Traveler with open mouths. Both were muscled, wiry men, tanned to the point of desiccation by hard outdoor work, and seemingly ageless because of it; they could have been forty or sixty.

The priest had the wrinkled face of a seventy-year-old to go along with the dark, shining eyes of a Rasputin. One side of his mouth turned up when he greeted Traveler; the other side of his face remained slack, probably the result of the long nasty scar that ran down the length of one cheek.

"You must be Mr. Martin," the priest said. "Miz Odegaard told us to expect you. You've arrived just in time for noon services. I hold them here because my church is boarded up."

"It hasn't been your church for years," one of the miners said. "Kennecott owns it lock, stock, and pew."

"God is not for sale, not even to Kennecott Copper." The priest offered his hand. "I'm Joe Balic. Everybody calls me Papa Joe. My critic here is Milo Popovich. His brother dissenter is Saso Marovich. They were all the congregation I had until you arrived."

"Nobody goes to church anymore," Popovich said and nodded at Marovich who immediately added, "That's why God gave us television."

Their grins said this was a ritual litany, a way of priming the priest.

"We've lost our fear of God," Balic responded. "It used to be, a man got old he started looking over his shoulder, feeling God breathing down his neck, getting ready to call him to account." As he spoke he walked back and forth in front of the Merc's glass display cases, following a path that had been worn into the pine floor over the years.

Marovich clicked his tongue. "The last time someone breathed down my neck it was one of the girls up at 520."

"It used to be a man paid for his sins," the priest continued. "I'm not talking about the likes of you, Saso, but rich men, important men, men who spent their lives stealing from the poor."

"Like Kennecott, you mean?"

Balic gestured impatiently. "Rich men hear footsteps behind them just like the rest of us. In our case, though, all we can do is pray and ask forgiveness. But men like Carnegie and Rockefeller, what do they do? They hear God sneaking up on them and they build libraries and set up foundations, trying to buy their way into heaven before it's too late. Now we've got people calling themselves born-again Christians who think making money proves that God loves them, and they don't share it with anybody."

"Do any of them make it to heaven?" Marovich said.

The priest smiled with the working side of his face. "Like Matthew said, 'It is easier for a camel to go through the eye of a needle, than for a rich man to enter into the kingdom of God.' "

"Maybe having your name on a library is all the immortality a man can get."

"That's a possibility, of course," the priest said. "If you can live with it."

The door opened and two men entered, followed by the young boy, Joe. The coppery smelter smell came with them, temporarily overriding the Bingham Merc's pine-resin, dry-goods atmosphere.

"Serbs," Popovich murmured under his breath.

Balic used the pretext of introducing Traveler to place himself between his two-man congregation and the new arrivals. "Mr. Martin, this is Sam Kuharic and Jake Selimovski."

They too looked like miners, fit, lanky men, but were at least a generation younger than Popovich and Marovich. Kuharic, the bigger of the two, pointed at Traveler and said, "Only a Croat would help an outsider."

"The mayor's wife sent him to us," Balic said.

Kuharic shook his head. "Ten minutes ago he poked his nose around up in Copperfield, looking for friends of ours, the Tempests."

"He looks like a cop to me," Selimovski added. "Maybe even a company cop."

"Bullshit," Popovich replied. "If anyone's spying for the company, it has to be a Serb."

Balic spread his arms like a referee, one hand against Selimovski's chest, the other holding back Popovich, and said, "Maybe you'd better explain your intentions, Mr. Martin."

"I'm here on personal business. It has nothing to do with Kennecott or the election."

"He looks like trouble," Kuharic said.

Balic nodded. "He's got a point."

"All I want to do is talk to the Tempests," Traveler said. "A few minutes will do."

"Garth Tempest worked with me at the mine before he hurt his leg," Kuharic said.

"We heard the stories about that accident," Popovich responded. "Self-inflicted, they say, but still he got workers' comp."

"Whatever you think about him, he's more of a friend than this guy," Kuharic said, indicating Traveler.

Father Balic elbowed some working room between the Serbs and Croats. "Garth Tempest still limps, otherwise he wouldn't have gone into clerking. Not that he's any better off than any of the rest of us now. The fact is, I'd say he's in worse shape, because the mine will still be here when all the stores are gone."

"I say we send this guy on his way," Kuharic said.

"Let him explain first," Balic answered.

Traveler knew better than to go with the truth—that he was there looking for a child named after him but who wasn't his. Looking from face to face, he saw no leeway, only men who'd been holding grudges forever, fighting the same battles their European ancestors had started centuries ago. If he fought them, no matter what the outcome, he'd have to leave town.

His best bet was to get the priest on his side. "You're right about God, Father Balic." Traveler dredged up a Sunday lesson memorized under his mother's watchful eye. " 'For thus saith the Lord, "I am merciful and gracious unto those who fear me." ' "

"Your good book is not mine," Balic said, "but fear's the key sure enough. Without it, I'm afraid, there is no faith."

"He's nothing but a white-head Mormon," Kuharic said.

The expected response was black-head, Traveler knew, sometimes nigger-head if it was a fight you wanted. He responded with a chuckle instead, to let them know he understood their joke, that for more than a century the men of Bingham Canyon had been calling Mormons white-heads, because Mormons left the dirty work to immigrant Gentiles rather than get their own hands and faces soiled in the mines.

He recited another of his mother's favorites. " 'And the servants of God shall go forth, saying with a loud voice: "Fear God and give glory to him, for the hour of his judgment is come." ' "

Nodding, the priest laid a hand on Traveler's shoulder. "I want you all to let this man be. We have enough trouble in this town already, what with everyone taking sides. If it's Garth Tempest you're looking for, he runs the Copper Keepsake souvenir shop up the street. Come on, I'll show you where to find him myself."

Father Balic took Traveler's arm. "Does anyone object?"

"Garth's not open," Kuharic said, "what with business being so bad."

"Humor me," Balic said.

The miners parted, Serbs on one side, Croats on the other, to let Traveler and the priest pass. As soon as they were outside on the sidewalk, the priest sighed deeply. "It's not Garth you seek, is it? Otherwise, you would have come right out with his name."

Traveler said nothing.

"If I find out you're causing trouble, I won't hold them back next time."

No more Sunday lessons came to mind, so Traveler settled for a nod.

"Each year there are fewer and fewer of us here. Each year we die a little more. If Kennecott wins, their open-pit mine will eat away the mountains and there will be nothing left to show that we ever existed."

He pulled Traveler out into the middle of the empty two-lane street. "There was a time when traffic backed all the way to the tunnel, and parking was a nightmare, especially around 520 Main."

Balic looked up and down the street and shook his head. "Listen to me, an old man fit for nothing but the boneyard. Only that'll be gone too, won't it, shoveled up and thrown into the smelters along with everything else. Even consecrated ground counts for nothing when the ore's rich enough."

"I'm sorry I can't vote," Traveler said.

"It wouldn't do any good anyway. Take my advice now and go about your business before my friends inside decide to take their grievances out on you. If Garth's not at the shop, you'll find the Tempest place down on Hagland Alley. Theirs is the only house with a wire fence out front."

The priest turned away to point down Main Street. "Keep going past the Royal Laundry and Christ Apostles Grocery until you reach Freeman Gulch. Turn left there and Hagland will be the first street on your right. If Garth's not home, you be sure to talk to Hannah out front where the neighbors can see you."

NINETEEN

Hagland Alley was more like a tunnel than a road, wide enough only for one car and lined with unpainted wooden shacks built up against the crumbling curb. Near the end of the block, a few shacks, smaller than the rest, looking no more substantial than outhouses, had sacrificed square footage for front yards five feet deep. The fence that Father Balic had mentioned was two feet of sagging chicken wire strung between a line of flimsy wooden sticks. Behind the wire three young children, two boys and a girl, played on bare dirt. They stopped to gawk when Traveler arrived. The oldest boy looked to be six or seven, but the other one was the right age, about three. The towheaded girl seemed younger.

Traveler glanced at the houses on either side, saw no signs of life, and knelt down on his side of the fence to ask, "Is your mother home?"

The two youngest ones hung their heads, while the older boy cupped his hands around his mouth and shouted toward the open doorway. "Hannah!"

"What is it?" a woman called from inside. The doorway was in shadow and offered no glimpse of her or the house's interior.

"A man's here."

"Coming."

The woman who appeared in the doorway wore the same kind of loose-fitting flowered housedress that Traveler's mother had favored during house-cleaning chores. She looked too old to be the children's mother, Traveler thought at first glance, but when she stepped outside, what he'd taken to be gray hair turned blond in the sunlight.

The moment he stood up, revealing his size, she held out her hands toward the children, who immediately clustered around her.

"Mrs. Tempest?" he said.

Her confirming nod was barely perceptible.

He forced himself to look at her and not the boy. When she couldn't meet his gaze, he had the feeling that she knew who he was. Perhaps Claire had prepared her for his coming, describing Traveler or maybe even providing a photograph of him. If so, now was not the time to pretend his name was Martin.

"I'm Moroni Traveler," he said.

She sighed, her shoulders sagged. "I've been waiting for you a long time."

"Claire must have told you about me, then."

"She said you'd never be able to resist, that in the end you'd have to come looking. She said it wouldn't do me any good to hide."

Traveler allowed himself a glance at the youngest boy.

"There are cookies inside," Hannah told the children. "You can watch TV while you eat them." When they hesitated, she herded them gently across the threshold and closed the door after them.

"Does the rest of your family know about Claire?" Traveler said.

"I can see she didn't tell you everything."

"Claire never told anyone everything."

"I kept my promise to her. I want you to know that. I kept the name Moroni Traveler. Moroni Traveler Tempest."

"There's a resemblance," he said, surprised that he hadn't seen it immediately. The boy had Claire's slender frame, the same dark eyes and hair.

"Claire said you'd want the child for your own." Hannah blinked rapidly, raising tears.

"You're more of a mother than Claire ever was."

She stepped past Traveler to look down Hagland Alley toward Main Street. "My husband should be here any minute. What with business the way it is, he usually closes up shop and comes home for lunch. It used to be tourists flocked here on weekends, but these days nobody comes to Bingham to buy souvenirs."

"Are you asking me to leave?" Traveler said.

"Garth doesn't know about Claire or the money I paid to her."

The doorknob rattled. Before Hannah could reach it, the door opened and the little boy appeared, sucking his thumb and staring wide-eyed at Traveler.

"Say hello to the man, Marty."

Traveler smiled. Another Moroni renamed. His father would appreciate it, though Claire probably would have objected.

Marty flung himself against Hannah and clung there. When Traveler went down on his knees, the boy hid his face in the folds of his mother's housedress.

"I talked with Claire for a long time that day she gave me the child," Hannah said. "I never understood your relationship with her."

"Did she tell you I was the father?"

"It was never clear. She said you weren't your father's son, whatever that means."

The boy showed his face long enough to say, "Don't cry, Hannah."

"I'd better come back another time," Traveler said.

"The damage is done. Someone will have seen you talking to me by now." She wiped her eyes. "Please, I need to know about you and Claire. Your relationship."

Even as Traveler wondered if lies wouldn't be best for everyone he found himself saying, "We'd broken up long before she got pregnant. More than a year."

"Then the child isn't yours?"

He shook his head.

"Why did you come here, then?"

"My father wants a grandchild and there are times when I think Claire was as close as he's ever going to get."

"I know why you came," Hannah said. "You wanted to see Claire again. She told me you were one of those old-fashioned Mormons with half a dozen wives. She said she ran off because she refused to share you with the others. She said you wanted to take the baby away from her to be raised by one of the other wives."

"I'm not married."

Hannah nodded. "I can see that. Even at the time, I didn't really believe the story about your wives. I was separated from my own husband then, and living with my sister Mattie in Sugarhouse. The other two children are hers."

"Mattie," Marty picked up. "Mattie's coming to the picnic."

"You go back inside, dear, and watch TV with the others," Hannah said.

"I want to stay with you."

"I'll be there in a minute. If you're good, you can help me make the potato salad for the picnic. Shoo, now."

As soon as the boy was safely inside, Hannah said, "You may as well know all of it. I stayed with my sister nine months before coming back to my husband. That way I could tell him the child was his. God knows what he'll think when he hears your name is Moroni Traveler."

"I've been calling myself Martin ever since I got into town. You're the only one who knows who I am."

Fresh tears rolled from her eyes.

"I'll leave."

"Won't your father be disappointed?"

"He only wanted to make certain that his grandchild was happy. That's all I wanted, too."

"We don't have much money. You can see that for yourself. But I love my angel. I guess you could take us to court and win because I gave Claire money. It was only a dollar, but she said that made it legal, though I know better now."

"I think my father would be happy if he could just visit one of these days."

"He wouldn't talk to my husband, would he?"

"I'll make sure of that."

She looked toward Main Street again, then back at the house. "Tomorrow's Sunday. Why don't you and your father come to the picnic tomorrow? The whole town is getting together at the high school around noon. It will be a celebration or a farewell depending on how the vote goes. Just don't tell my husband who you are."

Traveler nodded. "We'll be there."

TWENTY

Traveler decided to rent a room for the night as a base of operations if nothing else. Emma Dugan's boardinghouse, two-stories of bleak clapboard the color of tarpaper, looked as if it were sagging between the derelict buildings on either side. Emma, too, seemed to sag as she greeted him at the door, until Traveler realized that the floor itself was out of plumb.

"You're Mr. Martin, aren't you," she said. She would have looked like a Norman Rockwell grandmother—gray hair in a bun, wire-rim glasses, a pigeon-shaped body wearing a hand-embroidered apron over her housedress—except for her shrewd, assessing eyes. "The mayor's wife told me to expect you. Let's get everything out front first, though, young man. I charge twenty-five dollars a day, in advance, breakfast and dinner included."

He counted out the money, which she tucked into an apron pocket before ushering him into a small living room filled with Victorian furniture and the aroma of lemon-oil polish. The door to a gleaming oak breakfront stood open. She reached in among the knickknacks, took out a Depression glass bowl filled with keys, and rooted among them until she found one with an attached label.

"I go to bed early," she said, "so you'll need this to get in the front door if you stay out past eight."

"I'll try not to disturb you."

"I'm putting you upstairs, so I'd appreciate it if you took off your shoes after eight o'clock."

He nodded.

"Since you got here too late for breakfast, I could fix you lunch."

"I'd like to make a phone call first."

A whistle sounded, distant but loud enough to be heard up and down Bingham Canyon.

"It's three o'clock," Emma said. "Hold on to something."

She closed the breakfront door and stretched herself against its curved glass like a mother protecting a child. When Traveler didn't move, she pointed at a tallboy on the other side of the room. The house started shaking before he reached it.

"Every day it gets worse," she said, "Kennecott blasting at the open-pit mine on the other side of the mountain. And every day this place sinks a little more, just like I do."

She smiled and stepped away from the breakfront. "Gravity's weighing us both down."

"It's a wonder the whole town hasn't collapsed."

"Don't think we haven't lost a few places over the years. Most just get so bad they have to be condemned and torn down. Would you like to see your room now?"

The room was small, no more than ten by ten, with a single window facing the mountainside out back. Towels had been set out on the Victorian bed which, despite its massive oak headboard, looked too short for a man Traveler's size.

The bathroom was down the hall. Traveler relieved himself, washed the smelter grime from his face and hands, then left the house looking for a public phone.

Martin must have been waiting for the call, because he answered in the middle of the first ring. "Don't keep me in suspense, for Christ's sake. Do I have a grandson or not?"

"I found him, all right."

"Claire's Moroni?"

"Absolutely."

"What's he like?"

"You can see for yourself tomorrow. We've been invited to a town picnic. Moroni Traveler the Third will be there."

"How did you handle it?"

"I'm calling myself Mr. Martin as you suggested."

"What time?" Martin asked.

"Noon. Do you want me to drive into town and pick you up?"

"I'd rather you stay there and keep your eye on our future partner at Moroni Traveler and Sons. I'll rent a car."

"I've got a room at Emma Dugan's boardinghouse, 454 Main Street. Meet me there and we'll plan strategy."

TWENTY-ONE

Martin arrived early enough to have breakfast, for which Emma charged an additional two dollars and fifty cents, cheaper than Strums Cafe, she pointed out, which wasn't open anyway because this was picnic day at the high school.

"You're invited too," she added, while refilling Martin's coffee cup. "A widow woman like myself always appreciates company at her table. What about you, why didn't you bring your wife along?"

"I'm a widower myself."

"Now that you say it, I can see that for myself. Look at that button on your coat. It's ready to drop right off. You give it to me this minute and I'll take care of it."

The moment she went for needle and thread Traveler said, "She reminds me of Kary."

"Your mother couldn't sew."

"Why did you marry her?"

"Why did you take up with Claire?"

"You win."

Martin winked. "Old age has to be good for something. Now, as soon as I get my coat back, let's take a walk. Maybe we can pass by the boy's house. With any luck, I can get a look at him before the picnic."

"There are some problems. We'd better wait."

Martin sighed. "Let's hear it."

"Not here."

As soon as they were strolling up Main Street, with no other pedestrians in sight, Traveler explained the situation, that Garth Tempest thought the child was his and knew nothing of Claire.

"Christ," Martin responded. "Why did Mrs. Tempest keep the name Moroni Traveler?"

"She promised Claire."

"She sounds too good to be true."

"The boy looks like Claire."

"I hope that's all he inherited from her."

"You always said it was upbringing that counted, not genes."

They passed the Golden Rule Store, the Royal Chocolate Shop, and the Knight Hotel, now boarded up. At 520 Main Martin stopped and looked up at the empty, decaying building and shook his head.

"What kind of man is this Garth Tempest?"

"I don't know," Traveler said.

"We'd better find out before we go to that picnic."

"It's Sunday morning," Traveler pointed out.

"So let's find ourselves a church or something."

They found the Serbian Lodge, locked up, the abandoned LDS Ward House, and the Holy Rosary Catholic Church in Carr Fork, showing no signs of life. At ten they heard distant church bells but couldn't home in on them before the ringing stopped.

"I talked to a priest at the Bingham Merc yesterday," Traveler said. "A Father Balic. We could try there."

The Merc was closed, but Balic was sitting on the wooden

steps out front with one of the Serbian miners Traveler had met before, Saso Marovich, who was now wearing what appeared to be a lodge cap.

"This is my father," Traveler said, keeping names out of the introduction.

"Take a pew," the priest said.

"We'd like to speak with you alone if we could," Traveler said.

"I was on my way up to the high school anyway, to help set up picnic tables," Marovich said.

"We only need a few minutes of the father's time," Traveler said.

"Don't worry about it," the priest said. "If I know Saso, you've done him a favor. Now he won't have to listen to the rest of my sermon."

Marovich tipped his cap. "A man sees enough fire and brimstone when he works for Kennecott." He walked away whistling.

"Now," Balic said as Martin settled on one side of him, Traveler the other, "which of my sermons would you like to hear?"

Because Martin was closer to the priest's age, he took the initiative. "The subject we have in mind is Garth Tempest."

Balic stared at Traveler and said, "I thought you spoke with him yesterday."

"Only his wife."

The priest sighed. "Garth's not one of mine."

"Even so," Martin said, maybe you can tell us what kind of man he is."

"I'm not one to gossip without good reason."

"We need to approach him on a personal matter," Martin said.

The priest fingered the scarred side of his face. "Garth's sure to be at the picnic. You can meet him for yourselves there."

"Would he welcome outsiders?"

Balic smiled. "Both sides will be there. Company men and

those of us who want to stay on here where we spent our lives and where we have memories."

"Which side is Garth Tempest on?"

"He says he's for the town, but Kennecott has offered him good money for that souvenir shop of his, more than he'd ever get selling off his stock a piece at a time. At least that's what I hear. Of course, Garth's a relative newcomer. He only moved here a couple of years ago, so his roots are somewhere else."

"We need a more personal assessment," Martin said.

"I'll introduce you to him at the picnic. After that, my advice is to keep quiet and listen to what he has to say. I could be wrong, you know. He doesn't have to be a company man, or even the man he seems to be. Now, if you'll excuse me. Some of my older parishioners will need help getting to the picnic."

"What do you make of that?" Traveler said once the priest was out of sight.

"I don't think he likes Garth Tempest," Martin said. "I also think we'll be able to kill two birds with one stone. When I was researching the Chester Building at the Historical Society, I was told that their photo expert, Wayne Pinock, would be here at the high school today. He's been in town for the last three days, staying with the mayor, taking photographs, and interviewing people on videotape for an oral history of Bingham Canyon."

TWENTY-TWO

Bingham High, three stories of bleak brick augmented by square metal casement windows, looked more like an abandoned warehouse than a school. Like everything else in the canyon, the building backed up against the hillside. Cribbing, made of telephone-pole-size logs, rose steeply behind it to keep the slag dumps stable. The grounds surrounding the school were made of badly cracked asphalt showing waist-high weeds in the wider gaps.

The smelter haze, held close to the earth by an oppressive noonday sun, made Traveler's eyes water. There was no green anywhere, no playing field as such, only a neighboring lot where scorched weeds had been mown recently. Picnic tables, divided into two equal but separate clusters, one posted CITY-HOOD, the other KENNECOTT, took up one end of the lot. The other end, about the size of two basketball courts, had red, white, and blue balloons tethered to lanes of sawhorses that appeared to have been set aside for some kind of children's game. Between the lanes, a few men were lazily tossing a football back and forth. Nearby, children clustered around a clown shaping balloons into animals, half a dozen of which—dachshunds mostly—already floated from strings above their heads.

A refreshment stand built of two-by-fours covered with red, white, and blue crepe paper stood between the table groupings. Next to the stand, a wooden stage, no more than eight feet square, had been constructed of raw lumber and was equipped with portable speaker and microphone.

Traveler and Martin arrived fifteen minutes early, hoping to collar Balic and hold him to his promise of an introduction to Garth Tempest, but the whole town seemed to be there ahead of them, a hundred people at least, maybe more. They appeared to be equally divided between the two sets of tables. Only the children moved back and forth freely, constantly crossing between the political lines.

"Don't sit anywhere until we locate the Tempests," Martin said. "We don't want to pick the wrong side."

"You look for Father Balic," Traveler said. "I'll find the mayor's wife. We know which side she and her husband are on. Be sure to call me Mo, not Moroni."

"Mo and Martin, what a team!"

Traveler headed for the refreshment stand since it seemed to lie on neutral ground. Directly in front of it, two lines had been formed, one for beer that was being served from aluminum kegs, the other for soft drinks, both courtesy of Kennecott Copper according to discreet notices stapled to the crepe paper. A hand-lettered sign attached crookedly to a nearby tree stated that lemons for lemonade had been donated by Tuttle's Grocery.

When Traveler asked for lemonade he was told that the fruit had been handed out yesterday, so each family could make and sweeten its own batch. He settled for a can of root beer and began wandering around, drawing stares but no overt approaches.

When he found Ida Odegaard she was having her picture taken seated beside Father Balic on folding chairs in the neutral zone. As soon as the priest saw Traveler, he shook his head slightly and mouthed, "Not here yet."

The photographer adjusted a tripod while Martin whispered in his ear. A dozen or so men stood off to one side as if waiting their turn. Four of them wore white shirts, red bow ties, and suspenders to match.

At Traveler's approach, Martin backed off far enough to say, "This is Wayne Pinock from the Historical Society."

Pinock, a squat, bearded man with horn-rim glasses perched on the top of his head, acknowledged the introduction with a wave of his hand but didn't take his eye from the viewfinder.

"If we could have the mayor now," he said, repositioning his camera a quarter turn so that the high school building would show in the background, "I think future generations will thank us for the effort."

Mrs. Odegaard put her glasses on to look for her husband but spotted Traveler and made a face.

"To look at him, you wouldn't know he was my son, would you?" Martin told her.

She glanced from one Traveler to the other, then shook her head.

"I tried giving him coffee to stunt his growth," Martin said, "but it didn't work."

Smiling broadly, a heavyset balding man, one of those in red bow tie and suspenders, stepped forward to shake Traveler's hand. "I'm Almon Odegaard, the mayor." He mopped his sweating brow while looking Traveler up and down. "We could use you on our team."

"The man's waiting to take your picture," his wife said.

"Company men on one side and my team, made up of good Binghamites all, on the other," the mayor added before taking his place beside Father Balic. "You may be our best chance to beat them."

"No ringers," one of the other men said.

The mayor winked. "Anyone at the picnic can play."

"Play what?" Martin asked.

"A friendly game of touch football. Father Balic has agreed to referee. Isn't that right, Papa Joe?"

The priest nodded.

"I'm out of shape," Traveler said.

"You don't look it," the mayor said.

Pinock signaled for silence. "Smile."

The mayor obliged.

For the next few minutes, Pinock took a series of photographs, taking careful left-to-right notes as he posed various groups, including the mayor, city council members, businessmen, and prominent citizens. Throughout, Ida Odegaard stayed with the photographer, identifying prospective subjects and making certain the man from the Historical Society had their names spelled correctly.

The moment Pinock finished, the mayor, trailed by his wife and Father Balic, disappeared into the crowd, shaking hands as he went. The sound of cheers grew intense, punctuated by occasional boos.

As soon as the crowd of onlookers began dissipating, Martin collared Pinock. "This man has been here all week, Mo, recording for posterity."

"I should have been here sooner," Pinock said. "The town's practically dead already. Another couple of weeks and I'd have been out of luck."

"You think Kennecott's going to win, then?" Martin said.

Pinock wiped sweat from his eyes before repositioning his glasses from the top of his head to his nose. "Look around you. Would you rather live in one of these shacks or a nice ranch-style house down in the valley?"

The photographer dug his foot into the dusty soil. "Besides, we're literally standing on a fortune. A mountain range full of copper ore. So no matter what, the mining's going to continue. I'm not saying the vote might not go against the company, but in the end it won't make much difference."

"I'm not a great one for change," Traveler said.

"He inherited that from me," Martin added. "That's why we want your help with the Chester Building."

"I got the message you left at the Historical Society. Only then you were using the name Traveler. A few minutes ago I heard you call yourself Mr. Martin."

Pinock picked up his tripod, with the camera still attached, and carried it to the nearest empty picnic table. Traveler scooped up the man's equipment case and followed, as did Martin, carrying the brown-bag lunch Emma Dugan had supplied.

"Before the day's over, I'll be taking a shot of every table," Pinock said. "That ought to get us a record of just about everybody left in town."

"We can explain about the name," Traveler said.

Pinock concentrated on adjusting the leveling bubble built into his tripod. When he had it centered he stepped back and said, "I'm listening."

Traveler handed him a business card and explained that he and his father were conducting a discreet investigation in Bingham, which was true as far as it went.

"God knows why I believe you, but I do," Pinock said as soon as Traveler finished speaking. "As for the Chester Building, if it were up to me, I'd like to see it preserved as a landmark, but I know a losing cause when I see one. So does the Historical Society."

"That settles it," Martin said. "We're definitely up against the church. Which means we back off too, Mo."

"I'm going to preserve it on film, if that's any consolation. If everything goes as scheduled here in the canyon, I'm planning to get to the Chester Building in the next few days. Don't worry, though. Even if I get held up here for a while, the powers that be have promised me the Chester won't come down until I get a chance to shoot it."

"Our office is there," Martin said. "We don't like the idea of moving."

Pinock shrugged. "In order to be a landmark, it has to be listed on the official register or have some kind of historical significance. Remember the shopping center they were building down by the train station last year? When they started digging, they found an unrecorded pioneer cemetery. Now it's a state park."

"The Chester Building has Brigham Young on the ceiling," Martin said.

"The old mural, you mean. I've seen a lot of those fall to the wrecker's ball."

"They say Thomas Hart Benton painted it."

Pinock bent over his camera to look through the viewfinder at the picnic table, which now had children sitting on it, waiting for their photo to be taken. "Even if there's provenance, which I doubt, it wouldn't be enough to save the place. The fact is, that's why I do my job, recording history for future generations, because there's no profit in the status quo."

"What would a Thomas Hart Benton that size be worth?" Traveler asked.

Stepping back from his camera, Pinock lowered his glasses into place and stared at Traveler. "It's always possible that a painting could raise the price of the building so high they'd back off condemning it. I think that's what you're really asking. The trouble is, the church—and I'm not saying they have any vested interest there—is the richest in this country."

"Would you be willing to help us save the Chester Building?" Martin said.

"I record history, I don't make it. But I'll do one thing for you. When I get back to town, I'll check some of the old WPA photographs that have been donated to the Society and see if I can spot Thomas Hart Benton."

"It used to be the Gustavson Building in the old days," Martin said.

"We've got his photos, too," Pinock said, "but even if we could prove Rembrandt painted the mural, I don't know if it would do much good."

He turned his back on Traveler to concentrate on photographing the children.

"Come on," Martin said. "Let's see if we can find ourselves a relative."

The crowd had grown; lines at the refreshment stand were ten people deep. The air was filled with dust thick enough to taste. Traveler felt the beginning of a sunburn on the back of his neck.

Martin, seemingly unaffected by the heat, plunged through the crowd, but it was Traveler who saw the priest first, sitting at a picnic table on the CITYHOOD side. Hannah Tempest was next to him, which meant the rangy, dark-haired man facing her was probably her husband Garth. The children weren't at the table, which held two wicker hampers, several platters covered with aluminum wrap, and a gallon-size thermos surrounded by paper cups.

The priest waved the Travelers over.

"Martins, father and son," Balic said, "I'd like you to meet Garth Tempest and his wife, Hannah."

While the men were shaking hands, Hannah, wearing a housedress similar to the one Traveler had seen before, shifted to her husband's side of the table, allowing Traveler and Martin to squeeze onto the bench beside the priest.

"The Martins are doing a little genealogy research," Balic said. "They tell me they're looking for Tempests."

"I'm the only one here in Bingham," Tempest said. "As far as I know, we don't have any Martins in the family."

"Kary Tempest," Martin improvised. "Born in Sanpete County. Dead now, of course."

"Never heard of her. We're not Mormons in my family and don't search for the dead the way you people do."

Martin nodded. "We wanted a last look around Bingham anyway, before it's too late." He made a show of scanning the landscape. Only Traveler knew it was Marty his father sought.

"Bingham's not much of a town these days," Tempest said, "but it's still a shame to think that all this will be eaten up by the mine."

"We may beat them yet," Father Balic said.

Tempest shook his head. "A man's business can't survive without customers, despite what the mayor says. 'That souvenir shop's a good investment,' he tells me last year, so I sink in my savings. 'History's on our side,' he says. 'They don't call Bingham Canyon Old Reliable for nothing. While other mining towns have turned into ghosts, the ore here has never run out.' Well, I haven't struck it rich. The fact is, I haven't had so much as a customer inside my shop in a week."

"Your investment's safe enough, what with Kennecott's offer," Father Balic said.

"Most of it will go to pay off the mortgage."

Nearby, a cheer went up, followed almost immediately by amplified banjo music, "Camptown Races."

"Sing along," someone shouted.

A few people joined in, but most, Traveler included, couldn't remember the words.

"There's our mayor now," Tempest said.

Traveler swung around on the bench to see Almon Odegaard and three others, the men in white shirts and red suspenders, standing on the makeshift stage with a banjo player. Until that moment, he hadn't realized that the mayor's wife had the table directly behind them, where she was setting out plastic utensils and stacks of paper plates on a red, white, and blue paper tablecloth.

"They call themselves the Bingham Barbers," Tempest said. "Our mayor thinks that leading a barbershop quartet makes him a historian, 'a keeper of tradition and lore,' he calls himself. If you ask me, it's an excuse for singing dirty songs."

Tempest took a deep breath and spoke in a singsong voice. " 'She married a Mormon cowboy who understood his game / He knocked her up with a double stroke, now she's got—' "

"Garth," Hannah said. "Here come the children, so watch your mouth."

Marty, wearing jeans and a white T-shirt that had COPPER KEEPSAKE stenciled on it, was carrying a blue dachshund balloon; the older boy and the girl had red balloons shaped like elephants. The three children immediately crowded around the end of the picnic table, staring at the covered food, while Tempest introduced Hannah's sister, Hattie Snarr, and her husband, Lyman. Hattie had her sister's sun-streaked blond hair, plus her own faceful of freckles, and a smile that made Hannah, like everyone else, reciprocate. By smiling, Hannah erased ten years from her face and made Traveler realize that she was an attractive woman, camouflaged by both housedress and disposition.

Lyman Snarr had smile wrinkles to match his wife's. He deepened them to grin at Traveler and say, "You look familiar to me."

Before Traveler could answer, the quartet switched to a loud, vigorous rendition of "The Battle Hymn of the Republic," halting all conversation and saving Traveler a lie.

Martin took his eyes off the boy long enough to put his mouth against Traveler's ear. "He looks just like Claire. Garth's got the same coloring too, thank God. Hannah was lucky there. Otherwise, she'd never have gotten away with saying the child was his."

The music stopped and the mayor moved close to the microphone to make an announcement. "We're going to halt the entertainment for a while to wet our whistles. After that, we'll be choosing up sides for a touch football game. As of now, the able-bodied are drafted to help carry a beer keg over to the playing field."

Martin's head moved only a fraction of an inch, but Traveler understood the gesture. Football, even the touch variety, could turn into war when aided and abetted by alcohol and politics.

"That's my signal to leave," the priest said, shaking hands again. "In this heat, I've got to stoke up on liquid." He trotted off toward the refreshment stand.

Hattie shook her head at his retreating form. "You men and your football. I'd better go find Jesse and make sure he's brought his first-aid kit."

"Jesse's our oldest son," Snarr explained as soon as his wife left. "He finished his medical residency at the university hospital last year, on one of those government scholarships. They pay and he agrees to practice for three years in small towns like Bingham."

"He's by Hattie's first husband," Tempest put in.

"I adopted Jesse years ago," Snarr said. "Right after his father died. As far as I'm concerned he's my son."

Tempest shrugged.

"Here comes Shaky," Hannah said.

"Shit," Tempest said, glaring at the man who was shambling their way on the balls of his feet. "He always waits for the clergy to leave, so he won't have to listen to a sermon. He wouldn't hang around us, Hannah, if you'd stop feeding him."

"The town owes him," she said.

"My wife, the do-gooder."

When the man reached their table, his hands started shaking so badly he pinned them in his armpits.

Tempest winked openly. "What is it today, Shaky, the malaria again?"

The man nodded. "Got it in the Second War. Never have been the same since."

"Shaky Johnson used to be our deputy sheriff," Tempest said, "until the shakes got the better of him."

"Deputy Johnson took a bullet for this town," Hannah said. "In the line of duty." She opened one of the picnic hampers and took out a small flask. "There was a time when Shaky Johnson ruled with an iron fist. If someone stepped out of line, Shaky took care of it."

"I knew everything that was going on in this town." Johnson licked his lips. "I still do when I put my mind to it."

"What about it, Shaky?" Tempest said. "Are you going to make any arrests today?"

"Don't mock." Hannah handed Johnson the flask. After several swallows, he sighed, tucked the flask into his back pocket, and held out his hands, which were now steady. "You come back when you're hungry," Hannah told him.

Johnson nodded and trotted away.

"That's the last we'll see of him," Tempest said, "until the shakes come back."

Hannah shrugged. "I'd better start serving the kids." To Martin she added, "You're welcome to join us."

"Go ahead and feed the children," Tempest said. "The men won't be eating until after the game."

Hannah began uncovering platters, revealing fried chicken, potato salad, and a green Jell-O mold filled with chunks of pineapple and cottage cheese. She gave the children a peek of dessert, an apple pie, then wrapped it again to protect it against the rising dust.

"Look, Aunt Hannah," the older boy said, pointing to the next table, where Ida Odegaard was unveiling a three-layer chocolate cake large enough for a wedding.

"If I know Ida," Hannah said, "she's probably got another cake stashed under the table. She's known for her chocolate cakes, but won't share the recipe because it's a family secret."

"I heard that," Ida called over good-naturedly. "Tell your men to keep their hands off my cake. The kids get first dibs."

Martin leaned over to speak to Marty. "What's your favorite dessert?"

The boy blinked, then looked from Hannah to the chocolate cake and back.

"It's okay, honey," she told him. "You can have whatever you want."

Marty headed for the cake, which Traveler felt like doing himself.

"No you don't," Tempest called after him. "You come back here and sit down and eat your lunch first."

The boy obeyed instantly, as did the Snarr children; they all took seats on the bench as near to Hannah as they could get.

Snarr raised an eyebrow at his sister-in-law, movement only Traveler was in a position to see. Hannah answered with a twitchlike smile before tucking a large paper napkin into the collar of her little girl's dress. "That's my angel." The boys did the same with their own napkins.

Under the table, Traveler nudged his father to stop him staring at Marty.

Snarr said, "Are you going to play football with us?"

"It's too hot to play anything," Martin said.

Snarr started to reply but was interrupted by his wife's return with a gaunt young man in his late twenties who had dark circles under his eyes.

As soon as he was introduced to Dr. Snarr, Martin asked, "What's your professional advice about playing football in this kind of weather?"

The doctor squinted at the bright sky. "Heat prostration is always a possibility."

"It's the company versus the town," Snarr put in.

"In that case—"

"Jesse's been up all night trying to deliver Mrs. Gamble's baby," Hattie interrupted.

"Boy or girl?" Martin asked, glancing at Marty.

"It's still pending," the doctor said.

"If they'd held the picnic next week," Hattie said, "Jesse would have been reassigned now that Bingham's too small to rate its own hospital anymore."

The doctor's beeper went off. "That's it. I've got a feeling I'm about to deliver Bingham's last baby." He looked toward the playing field where the sawhorses were being repositioned along the sidelines. "I'll be back as soon as I can."

"Let me fix you a plate of food before you go," Hattie said.

He shook his head. "With Mrs. Gamble's cooperation I'll be back later to eat."

"Or set bones," Martin muttered.

"You're acting like old ladies," Tempest said. "What better way to work up an appetite than with a friendly game of touch football?"

"If you ask me, the Martins are the ones showing a little sense," Hattie said.

"I didn't ask you," Tempest said.

Lyman Snarr pointed a finger at his brother-in-law and was about to say something when Mayor Odegaard arrived, carrying a six-foot aluminum stepladder in one hand and a bullhorn in the other. "How's Mrs. Gamble?" he asked the doctor.

Jesse Snarr touched his beeper. "I'm on my way back to the hospital right now."

"You tell her for me, the town needs a Bible name for luck."

The mayor opened the ladder, set it next to the table, and sat on the second of its five rungs. "How about John if it's a boy?"

"I'll give her the message," the doctor said before hurrying away.

Odegaard tapped Traveler on the shoulder. "Hold the ladder for me, will you, young man?"

As soon as Traveler obliged, the mayor, still carrying his bullhorn, climbed onto the ladder's upper rung, a vantage point that gave him a bird's-eye view of the picnic area. "Come up a step," he said to Traveler, "and let me show you a few things about Bingham."

Gingerly, Traveler tested the ladder's stability before easing onto the first rung.

The mayor pointed toward the tables beyond the refreshment stand. "As you can see for yourself, we've got Croatians on one side, Serbs on the other, even though there's no consensus among them as to which way they're voting."

The Serbs, Traveler noticed, were wearing lodge hats, many so moth-eaten they looked generations old.

"Not many are company men I can tell you that, but they'll sure as hell take sides when we start playing football. I hear Father Jake's brought in some ringers, a couple of miners who used to play ball for Draper High School. That's why the town needs someone your size, to even things out. If you look close, money's changing hands right now. The company's a two-to-one favorite."

"With someone your size," Tempest told Traveler, "we might beat the odds."

"My money stays in my pocket," Odegaard said.

"What do you say, Mr. Martin?" Tempest asked. "Give us a hand. We can get to know each other better that way."

Traveler glanced at his father for advice, but he had his eyes on the boy.

"In the old days," the mayor said, "we could have used old Killum-Cow Charlie on our side. He was a local strongman who used to work Bourgard's slaughterhouse down in Frogtown."

Shouts erupted from the refreshment area where two big men, one a priest, were climbing onto the makeshift stage.

"That's Father Jake Bannon and Frank Murdock," the mayor said. "They're hand-in-glove with the company, Murdock because he owns a lot of land, and Father Jake because he wants to move on to bigger things in Salt Lake. Jake played ball for Notre Dame, second-string but still better than anybody we've got. We're going to get creamed out there without help."

Even from a distance, Father Jake looked impressive, at least thirty pounds heavier than Traveler, who'd slimmed down since his playing days.

"What's it to be?" Odegaard said. "Everybody has to choose sides. I'm quarterbacking for the home team."

Traveler stepped off the ladder.

"You go ahead, son." Martin raised an eyebrow in Tempest's direction. "I'll stay behind with the women and children and root for you."

Against his better judgment, Traveler shrugged his acceptance.

"Good man." The mayor raised the bullhorn to his lips and announced, "Gentlemen, let's play some football."

TWENTY-THREE

While Traveler stood on the sidelines drinking beer with his new teammates, the opposing co-captains, Mayor Odegaard and Garth Tempest representing the city, and Father Bannon and Frank Murdock for the company, met in the middle of the dusty field to watch Father Balic toss a coin. The sun, though past its zenith, felt hotter than ever. The air was filled with gnats rising from the newly mown weeds underfoot. The playing area itself couldn't have been more than forty yards long and twenty wide.

Traveler knelt to pick foxtails from his jeans before rolling his cuffs ankle high.

Beside him, Lyman Starr did the same. "Officially Kennecott isn't represented here," Snarr said, "only those who favor selling out to them."

"Do any of them work for the company?" Traveler asked.

"Like the mayor said, some are miners. Some work at the smelter, but they're only company men in the sense that Kennecott pays their wages. It's really the town that's divided."

Traveler double-tied the laces on his running shoes. "You

can't blame people for wanting to sell out and make money."

"I'm a renter myself. But there are those who say the company is trying to get things cheap."

Out on the field Father Balic, who'd exchanged his priestly robes for jeans and a short-sleeve Hawaiian-style shirt, supervised the shaking of hands, then dramatically flipped a silver dollar high into the air. When it landed, the mayor raised his bullhorn. "Cityhood wins the toss."

A moment later, Balic waved his arms, signaling all players to join him on the field. As soon as everyone had gathered around him, Balic said, "Here are the rules. We're going to play for thirty minutes, including the timeouts for beer, which I will call personally. Whoever's ahead at the end of thirty minutes wins. I'll start my watch as soon as we kick off and let it run. There will be no first downs. You get four plays to score or kick. One other thing, Father Bannon's team is short a man, so Garth Tempest has volunteered to fill in."

Tempest, Traveler noticed suddenly, was gnashing his teeth.

Traveler leaned close to Snarr. "What's up with your brother-in-law?"

"Shit. I know that look. He's probably gloating about the prospect of knocking me on my ass."

"I get the feeling it's me he's after."

Snarr shook his head. "He's a mean drunk, but not dumb enough to take on someone your size. Me, he tries to bully every chance he gets."

"He's only had a couple of beers."

Even as Traveler spoke, the teams headed for the beer keg and one last pregame thirst quenching.

"Once we start," Father Balic said, raising his paper cup in a toast, "you men can come out of the game for a beer whenever you want, but the rest keep on playing."

Over the top of his cup, Traveler watched Garth Tempest, who appeared to be staring back.

"Let's get going," the mayor said. "The women are waiting." He handed his bullhorn to Father Balic and led his team onto the field.

The kickoff went to the mayor personally, who was tackled after a short gain.

"I thought we were playing touch," Traveler said in the huddle.

"We are," the mayor said, "but you can't dispute a tackle."

Traveler sighed. The pudgy Mayor Odegaard had to be forty-five at least and was already breathing hard. Looking around the huddle, Traveler realized he stood out as the biggest man, as did the Catholic priest on the other team.

"Do you want to carry the ball?" the mayor asked.

Traveler shook his head. "It's easier to pass on a field this size. I'll stay in to block for you."

At the line of scrimmage, the priest, wearing a Notre Dame sweatshirt with the sleeves cut off to reveal intimidating biceps, lined up opposite Traveler. Tempest was facing his brother-in-law, as Snarr had predicted.

Traveler took no aggressive action but merely got in the priest's way long enough for the mayor to throw his pass. The ball sailed thirty yards into the end zone for a touchdown, much to Traveler's surprise.

The mayor immediately left the game for a beer, which left the team one man short on defense. Even so, Traveler made only a perfunctory move to get by the priest and rush the passer. The company quarterback didn't have much of an arm and had to settle for ten-yard passes. Even so, he moved his team within striking distance on its final down.

As they lined up for the play, the priest grinned at Traveler and muttered, "Mormon pussy."

The comment so surprised Traveler that he failed to sidestep the priest's block and landed on his backside, with the priest on top, jabbing a deliberate elbow into Traveler's ribs.

"Touchdown!" Father Balic called.

Traveler got up slowly, smiling to cover his pain. *If they see you're hurt,* his pro coach, Bart Siddons, used to say, *they'll be on you like wolves. If you want to survive, you have to get mad and get even.*

Traveler took a deep breath. He had no intention of getting

mad. All he had to do was watch himself. The priest, despite his biceps, wasn't that good.

The mayor came back in the game for the kickoff, reeking of beer and looking a bit red in the eyes. This time, the mayor moved out of the way so someone else could handle the kickoff. Traveler made one block for the runner, who cut the wrong way and lost yardage.

"Time out!" Father Balic hollered through the bullhorn. "Beer break."

Traveler settled for water, while the others gulped enough beer to make them slosh.

When play resumed, the mayor called another long pass before moving them to the line of scrimmage. Traveler found himself facing Garth Tempest, while Father Bannon had switched to Lyman Snarr. As a result, the priest flattened the mayor before he had time to throw and Traveler found himself trying to fend off punches worthy of a street-fighter.

Traveler took a shot on his shoulder before pinning Tempest's arms. "I know you're drunk," Traveler whispered in the man's ear, "but don't push it."

He looked around for the referee, but Father Balic was on the sidelines drinking beer.

"You don't scare me," Tempest said once he was on his feet.

When Traveler nudged him toward his teammates, Tempest tripped, which caused the priest to rush Traveler, coming nose-to-nose to say, "If you want to shove somebody, try me."

Play with anger. Coach Siddons's words echoed inside Traveler's head. *Hate them. They're the enemy. It's the only way you'll survive as a linebacker in professional football.*

Traveler backed away.

The priest turned around to slap hands with Tempest.

In the huddle Traveler saw that Lyman Snarr had a bloody nose from trying to stop Father Bannon's last pass rush. The mayor was patting the dust from the seat of his pants; his hair was matted with foxtails.

"I need more time to throw," he said.

The other players, Snarr included, avoided Traveler's eyes.

"I'll take the priest," he said.

Snarr wiped his nose. "Thank God."

"Keep an eye on your brother-in-law," Traveler told him.

On the next play, Tempest blindsided him, the kind of clip that could tear up a knee, while the priest rammed a forearm into the side of Traveler's head. Pain blinded him momentarily while instinct, fueled by years of practice, tucked him into a protective ball enabling him to roll with the blow. He came up limping and grinding his teeth. *Use the pain. Steep yourself in it.* Adrenaline started his hands shaking.

"Are you okay?" the mayor said.

Traveler nodded. Sweat stung his eyes but he refused to wipe them as he turned his back on the opposition and joined the huddle. Only then did he realize that the mayor had completed a pass halfway down the field.

"Sorry about Garth," Snarr said. He had a cut ear to go along with his bloody nose. "I couldn't stop him."

Traveler glanced back to see Tempest watching him from the new line of scrimmage. The man's wild-eyed look was the same one Traveler had seen in the mirror on game days.

"Listen up," the mayor said. "Keep them off me one more time and I'll put it in the end zone for sure."

Snarr groaned.

As they moved to the line of scrimmage, Traveler studied the opposition. Tempest looked crazy, while Bannon merely acted cocky. Take the priest out and he'd be slow to recover, if at all. Chances were Tempest would have to be disabled totally before he'd let up.

"I'm going after Notre Dame first," he whispered to Snarr. "Protect yourself."

Bannon and Tempest switched places at the last minute, leaving Snarr to face the priest as the ball was snapped. Traveler used Tempest's momentum to hurl him aside, then cracked back on Bannon from behind, strictly illegal but effective. The priest could walk afterward, but only with a limp. From then on, he just went through the motions, allowing Traveler to concentrate on Tempest. By the end of the game, Tempest was lining up as far from Traveler as possible.

Someone fired a pistol and Father Balic gathered both teams around the beer keg to declare the game a tie. Wives began mingling with the sweaty, grime-covered players, handing out wet paper towels and Band-Aids. Hattie Snarr shook her head at her husband's plight before going to work on him. Traveler went through half a dozen towels before the last one came away from his face in a reasonably clean condition.

Cups brimming with foamy beer were handed out for a toast.

"To Bingham," the mayor said. "May her memory never die."

"To Bingham High," someone shouted.

Someone started to sing, to the tune of "Dixie":

> "My heart's in love with our good old Bingham,
> Copper mountains, and girls in gingham.
> So I pray
> Let me stay,
> Let me stay
> In Bingham town."

Others joined in.

> "Then let me stay in Bingham, hooray, hooray.
> With Bingham's band I'll take my stand,
> To live and die in Bingham.
> Away, I'll pray, to stay out West in Bingham."

The moment the song ended Hattie took her husband by the hand and led him off in the direction of the picnic area. Traveler was about to follow when Father Bannon, still limping, came over and held out his hand.

"Sometimes I'm an asshole," he said.

Traveler shook the man's hand.

"Now I know why I was second-string," Bannon said.

"We're going to pay for it tomorrow with aching muscles," Traveler said.

"I used to watch you play for Los Angeles. That's why I got carried away out there."

Christ, Traveler thought, looking around to see if anyone was eavesdropping. Now was not the time to have his real name circulated. "I shouldn't have gotten mad. Hell, I shouldn't have played."

The priest shook his head and grinned. "I wouldn't have missed playing against you for anything."

"I don't think Garth Tempest would agree."

"The man shouldn't drink, that's for sure. Hell, he probably won't remember a thing when he sobers up."

Traveler looked for Tempest in the crowd but couldn't find him. He did catch Martin's eye and signaled for help.

"I could talk to Garth if you'd like," Bannon said.

Traveler shrugged. "I'll be gone tomorrow."

"What brought you to Bingham anyway?"

"Nostalgia as much as anything else."

"I figured you for a friend of the mayor's."

"I'm not here to take sides, if that's what you mean."

Martin arrived, carrying Marty on his shoulder. Once introductions had been made, Martin said, "I'm sorry to break things up, but they're waiting lunch for us."

"Again, my apologies." The priest shook Traveler's hand a second time. "Playing against you was an eye-opener, that's for sure."

As soon as the priest was out of earshot, Martin said, "He recognized you, didn't he?"

Traveler nodded. "Where's Garth?"

"He had to go to the bathroom," Marty said. "That's when Hannah sent us to find you."

"Get us a couple of fresh beers and meet us back at the table," Martin said. "I'm in no mood for lemonade."

"I want some of Aunt Ida's cake," the boy said.

"Let's go, then," Martin said.

144

"Giddyup," Marty shouted and dug his heels into Martin. Martin trotted away, whinnying like a horse.

Traveler bypassed the keg on the field in favor of the refreshment stand, where he had only a short wait. He drank one beer immediately, then managed to carry six back to the table.

"Excuse the fingers," he said, setting cups on the table. "It was the only way I could handle so many."

Hannah, Hattie, Lyman, and Martin had full plates in front of them. Garth was missing.

"You needn't have brought so many," Hannah said. "Garth's not feeling well and the rest of us are sticking to lemonade."

"He's hung over," her sister said. To her husband she added, "Left on your own, you would be, too."

The children had abandoned their own table to sit with the Odegaards, who were in the process of handing out pieces of chocolate cake.

"We're going to play family games later on," Hattie said.

"No more for me," her husband pleaded.

"And after that there's singing and fireworks."

Traveler and Martin didn't get away until after dark. By then Martin had consumed too much beer to drive back to Salt Lake.

"I hope your landlady will let me stay," he said as they crossed Main Street toward the boardinghouse.

Traveler ached all over. Each deep breath triggered a stab of pain from his rib cage. "I'd feel better if we were leaving right now."

"It would be nice to see Marty again, though, wouldn't it?"

"We'd better leave well enough alone. Tempest may be a bastard but he's the only father he knows."

"Hannah's a good woman, too," Martin said.

"No good-byes, then."

Martin sighed. "It would have looked good, MORONI TRAVELER AND SONS on the door."

TWENTY-FOUR

Sound woke Traveler. He opened his eyes to dawn, feeling his father next to him in the narrow pioneer bed, ignoring the need to stretch because there was no room. He yawned, a mistake which started his rib cage throbbing.

The sound, a knock at the door, repeated itself. "Mr. Martin!" Emma Dugan called out. "Are you all right?"

Martin groaned.

"There's been an outbreak of food poisoning," the woman shouted.

Traveler shook Martin.

"I heard her, for Christ's sake. I'm not poisoned, only exhausted. What time is it?"

"Six-thirty." Traveler swung his legs over the side of the bed, found yesterday's underwear and jeans, and pulled them on. Martin stayed where he was.

"Mr. Martin!"

"Coming." Barefoot, Traveler hurried to the door and opened it. "As you can see, Mrs. Dugan, we're fine."

"I was afraid you might have eaten something bad at the picnic."

"We had your sandwiches," Traveler said, though they were still uneaten and in their brown bag on the nightstand.

"I saw you sitting with the Tempests," she said.

"Hannah made fried chicken and potato salad," Martin said from the bed. "Who could resist?"

Mrs. Dugan shook her head. "You two men get yourselves over to the hospital right now and have yourselves checked. It must have been the mayonnaise. You know how it gets in the heat and sun. The Tempests and the Snarrs are all down with it."

Martin said, "What about the children?"

"As of now only the grown-ups are real sick. The kids are more frightened than anything else. But you know what they say about food poisoning. It can strike you days later. That's why you'd better get yourselves looked at. Besides, some of the other men who played ball are sick too. That's why I rushed up here to see if you were all right."

Martin got out of bed wearing only his shorts, then turned his back to pull on his trousers.

Traveler repeated, "How bad, Mrs. Dugan?"

"I only know what I hear, but there's a rumor that they're dead already, and that they're keeping it quiet to prevent a panic. That's why I'm going over to the hospital right now and see if there's anything I can do. We've only got one doctor, you know, Jesse Snarr. Him being a Snarr, we can thank the Lord he didn't get hit with the poisoning too."

"We're coming with you," Martin said.

"Coffee's ready in the kitchen. You can drink a cup on the way."

The morning was warm, seventy degrees at least, despite Bingham's six-thousand-foot altitude and surrounding mountain peaks that were still shielding the town from the rising sun. By the time they reached the hospital, a crowd as large as the one attending the picnic had gathered out front. Mayor Odegaard, flanked by Father Balic and Father Bannon, was standing on the steps of the bleak, unpainted gunite building, signaling for a silence that was already in effect.

"A helicopter landed down at the high school at first light," the mayor said. "Maybe you heard it. An emergency medical team was on it. They're inside now, helping out Doc Snarr."

Traveler and Martin stayed at the back of the crowd, while Mrs. Dugan began working her way forward.

"Has anyone heard about the children?" Martin whispered to a woman in front of him.

She half turned to say, "The poor things are practically orphans."

Before he could ask another question, she put a finger to her lips and nodded in the mayor's direction.

Odegaard addressed the crowd. "There's been a lot of wild talk in the last few hours, so Doc Snarr asked me to brief you on the situation. After I do, I expect everyone to go home. We can't have you blocking Main Street, in case we have to bring in an ambulance. Besides, the noise out here isn't doing the patients any good either, that's for sure. Now, the situation is this. Hannah Tempest and her sister, Hattie, are both in critical condition, but holding their own, the doctors say. Garth Tempest and Lyman Snarr are feeling a little better this morning and are listed in stable condition. Young Marty's sick too, but it may only be the excitement or too much rich food. We're hoping for the best."

"What about company men?" a man asked, not a shout but loud enough to heard clearly. "Are any of them sick?"

"That's the kind of thing we're trying to avoid. It's a case of food poisoning, pure and simple, nothing to do with the election."

"We're down four votes," the same man said.

"We heard it was a mass poisoning," someone else put in.

The mayor held up his arms. "I'm standing here, aren't I? Now go home and stop spreading rumors. We'll post bulletins on the door of city hall every few hours."

While the crowd dispersed, Traveler and Martin retreated to the doorway of an abandoned hardware store. A moment later Shaky Johnson passed them, hesitating in midstride as if about to panhandle, then seemed to recognize them and continued on his way.

"Hold it," Martin shouted after him.

As soon as Johnson retraced his steps, Martin gave him a five-dollar bill.

"Someone asked me to pass it on to you," Martin explained to the bewildered-looking man. "Said he owed it to you for a long time but was embarrassed for taking so long to pay it back."

Johnson leaned close. "You're lawmen, aren't you? I can tell by your eyes. By God, I haven't lost my touch yet. If you need anything, you come to Shaky. Most times you can find me down at the Pastime Bar."

"We'll do that."

After a quick nod, Johnson trotted away.

"I could use a drink myself," Martin said, "to steady my own hands." He mimicked Shaky.

"Stop playing Good Samaritan and concentrate on food. We were sitting at the picnic table, eating the same things as everyone else. We should be sick too."

"So should the other two kids."

Traveler closed his eyes and saw the picnic table again, the platter of fried chicken, the Jell-O ring, the potato salad, all of which he'd sampled liberally.

"I ate everything," he said.

"So did I."

"Maybe the food went bad later, after we'd gone. It had been sitting in the sun long enough."

"I want to see Marty for myself."

"Let's talk to the mayor first."

The crowd was down to half a dozen, though Almon Odegaard was still guarding the hospital door. He didn't look happy to see Traveler or Martin.

"We heard some of the other football players had been taken sick," Traveler said to explain their presence.

"We thought so at first," the mayor said. "But it was nothing worse than hangovers and hysteria."

"We were sitting at the Tempests' table," Martin said.

"I remember," the mayor said. "But you look healthy enough. I'll have one of the emergency crew examine you if you'd like."

"What are the symptoms?"

"You'd know if you had them," Odegaard said. "Vomiting and severe diarrhea. The women are comatose."

"Maybe the food went bad later," Martin said. "Maybe they took it home from the picnic and had a snack."

"Before Hannah lost consciousness, she told Doc Snarr she knew better than to keep the potato salad after it had been sitting in the sun. Even so, we're keeping a close eye on the other two children in case we've missed something."

"Who's looking after them?" Martin said.

"It's kind of you to ask," the mayor said. "Once the docs are through with them, they'll be staying with us. Our own are grown up and moved away now."

"If you need help, or money, all you have to do is ask."

The mayor stared at Martin, then raised his head to study Traveler's face. "You never did explain your connection with the Tempest family."

"We thought we might be related."

"And are you?"

"Not by blood."

TWENTY-FIVE

The Pastime Bar reminded Traveler of the Depression-era photos he'd seen in old *Life* magazines. Everything looked worn out; the woodwork, the plate-glass window, even the unlit neon sign had faded to shades of gray. If it hadn't been for the open door and the smell of rancid beer, he would have thought the place was abandoned.

Inside, the only customer, Shaky Johnson, was standing in front of a long brass-railed bar showing his quick-draw move to a bored-looking bartender, who perked up at the sight of Traveler and Martin.

"Welcome," he called as they crossed the wood-planked floor, avoiding scattered piles of mildewed sawdust along the way. The room, as long and narrow as a railroad car, was empty except for a jukebox in one corner and a small table in the other.

"What are you drinking, Shaky?" Martin asked.

"Beer's all that's legal in this state." Johnson winked.

"We'll have whatever's legal, then, for everybody."

"Four Shaky specials coming up." The bartender set up

boilermakers, using brim-full double-shot glasses for the whiskey. "Here's to our last deputy."

Traveler sipped, as did Martin, while Johnson and the bartender downed their shots in quick, greedy gulps. After a deep shuddering sigh, Johnson put down his glass and held out a rock-steady hand.

Smacking his lips, the bartender wrapped a hand around the bottle and looked to Martin for instructions. Martin's nod set him in motion, topping off all four shot glasses.

"Well now," Johnson said, "I can see I was right about you two. You came here to pick a deputy's brains. Am I right?"

"Retired deputy," the bartender added.

Johnson tapped the side of his nose. "Once a lawman, always a lawman. You never lose your instinct." He pointed a finger at Traveler. "I never forget a face, and yours I remember from somewhere."

"Maybe we ought to sit down and talk about it," Martin said.

Johnson nodded. "I take your meaning. You need a little privacy." He gestured toward the bartender. "If you give the okay, Vince here can set himself up another bottle so he won't feel left out."

As soon as Martin dropped a twenty-dollar bill on the bartop, Johnson carried the open bottle to the table in the far corner. Traveler and Martin brought the beer mugs and shot glasses.

Once Johnson seated himself, he checked his hand for steadiness, apparently spotted a tremor in the offing, and downed another whiskey. "My guess is you wouldn't be here unless you wanted to know about the poisoning."

Traveler looked at his father, who raised an eyebrow in return. Their intent, considering Shaky's state, had been to get an assessment of Garth Tempest's character and qualifications as a father.

"Don't listen to the talk, that's my advice," Johnson said. "Kennecott's richer than the Arabs, so they wouldn't be killing people to get the land, most of which they own already. Hell, you must know the law as well as I do. In this state, mining companies can use eminent domain to condemn anything that gets in their way. Bingham's in their way at the moment. So no matter how the vote goes, it's only a matter of time."

He stamped the floor with his foot. "We're sitting on ten million tons of copper ore. With that kind of money at stake, us chickens don't have a chance. Of course, it could have been some hothead, thinking he was doing Kennecott a favor by taking out some of the voters for tomorrow's election."

"That doesn't make sense," Martin said. "It's the mayor who's leading the fight against Kennecott. He's the logical target."

"The Snarrs and Tempests add up to more votes. With the town shrinking the way it is, four could turn the tide."

"Why not the mayor, too, then, and a few others to make certain of the count?"

"You're right. I must be slipping." Johnson examined his hands, which were steadier than Traveler's at the moment. "It was Garth Tempest who started the rumors about company murder, you know. Not that I blame him, sick and half out of his head the way he was. Hell, if I'd been in his place, I'd've thought Kennecott was after me for sure."

"Are there any other rumors we ought to know about?" Traveler said, refilling Johnson's glass.

"Up at the hospital, they say Miz Tempest and Miz Snarr might not make it."

"And their husbands and the little boy?" Martin said.

"They say men are tougher than women, but I've never believed it until now."

"What do you know about the Tempests and the Snarrs?" Traveler said.

Johnson took a mouthful of beer and swished it around like mouthwash before swallowing. "They're relative newcomers to the canyon, so I didn't know them when I was a deputy. That's when you get to see people at their worst, when you're working for the law. As far as I know, they're decent people. Garth's a bit of a hothead and not too smart, sinking his money into that souvenir shop when things were already going to hell in a handbasket around here. Lyman Snarr, now, he works the mine, so his paychecks ought to be regular enough."

Johnson snapped his fingers at Traveler. "I knew I recognized you. You're a football player. Moroni something, named for an angel and kicking ass in the pros. Am I right?"

Traveler nodded.

"I must be losing it, taking you for a lawman."

Traveler glanced at Martin, who rolled his eyes and said, "I can't see it makes any difference now." He handed Johnson a business card.

Johnson read it and clicked his tongue. "Thank God. My nose is still working. Private lawmen are better than nothing."

Traveler said, "It might be best if we kept this conversation to ourselves."

"Mum's the word. Safe as houses, that's me as long as I haven't got the shakes."

"What does it take to keep you steady?"

"A bottle a day keeps the doctor away."

Traveler set up a weeklong, paid-up account with the Pastime's bartender before he and Martin left. They were halfway to Emma's boardinghouse before he said, "I'm not coming back to town with you."

"You're damn right. Someone's got to stay here and look after Marty's interests until he and his parents are out of the hospital."

"And if they don't get out?"

Martin shook his head. "I'd stay with you if I didn't have an appointment at the City and County Building tomorrow morning. That's when my contact is running a computer check on the Chester Building."

TWENTY-SIX

An east wind off the Great Salt Desert cleared the air in Bingham Canyon the next morning, pushing the smelter fallout toward Salt Lake City. The thermometer in Emma Dugan's kitchen read seventy-six degrees as Traveler sat down to a bowl of oatmeal at seven A.M.

"The radio says ninety by noon," Emma told him. "My bones tell me ninety-five. If you don't mind, I'm going to leave you here alone for a while and go vote early, before it gets too hot."

"Why don't I walk with you as far as the hospital?" He started to get up but she waved him back into his chair.

"It's a sin to waste perfectly good food, young man. I can wait a few minutes until you finish."

The oatmeal, laced with brown sugar and butter, soothed his stomach.

"I took a casserole over to the Odegaards last night," Emma said as she poured him coffee. "There till all hours, I was. I couldn't bear to leave those poor children. Young Dr. Snarr did drop by before I left, but he didn't have good news. Hannah and Hattie are still unconscious. If you ask me, the doctor's going to make himself sick if he doesn't get some rest. There are plenty of volunteers, myself included, but he won't leave his mother's side except to see the children."

She took Traveler's empty bowl and began rinsing it in the sink. "Father Bannon is opening his church for special prayer services this morning. The old place was already boarded up, but he went out last night and pulled the planks off the door himself. You're welcome to join me there after I vote."

"I appreciate the invitation."

A church bell rang in the distance.

"Dear God," she said, dropping the plate and breaking it. "That's too early for services. It means bad news, young man. We'd better get going."

A good-size crowd had gathered in front of the Holy Rosary Catholic Church by the time Traveler and Emma arrived. Mayor Odegaard, already wearing a black armband, stood in the bed of a pickup truck, hands raised in a gesture of patience, unable to speak until the bells stopped ringing. The church's double doors stood wide open. All but one window, the one nearest to the peak of the church roof, had been nailed over with plywood sheets so badly weathered they must have been in place a long time.

Shaky Johnson, wearing a service cap and looking steady and reliable, was stationed at the rear of the truck, his back against the tailgate, his arms folded as if he were on duty again. Traveler nodded at him, but the man refused to be distracted.

The bells slowed, then stopped, though their echo continued up the canyon for several seconds. By the time the sound died away, Father Bannon and Father Balic appeared in the church's doorway, wiping the sweat from their faces. At a nod from Father Bannon, the mayor said, "As most of you know already, Hannah Tempest has passed on."

"Sweet Jesus," Emma murmured, crossing herself. "Her

poor husband, and that dear little child. To lose a mother so early."

"I'm sorry to say," the mayor continued, "that Hattie Snarr has been put on life support and is in very critical condition. Her husband and the little boy have taken a turn for the worse too, though Garth Tempest seems to be holding his own, thank God. We can also be thankful that no one else has been stricken."

"Amen," Emma said.

"Doc Snarr is getting ready to transfer the survivors to the hospital in Salt Lake. In the meantime, Father Bannon and Papa Joe Balic ask that you come inside and join us in prayers for their recovery."

When some people hesitated the mayor said, "All faiths are welcome."

Emma touched Traveler's arm and said, "Are you coming inside?"

"There's something I have to do first."

"Us Catholics aren't devils, despite what you Mormons think."

He hated misrepresenting himself at a time like this, but now was not the moment for confession.

She stood on tiptoe to look him in the eye. "You have your own devils, I can see that in your face." She joined the crowd filing inside.

Claire had been a great one for devils, too. *Never cross the threshold of a Catholic church,* she said whenever they passed one. *The devil lives inside, just waiting to get hold of one of us Saints so he can drag us down to hell.*

Traveler's mother had her own variation. *All Catholics work for Satan. They do his bidding and steal bad little boys and girls. Do you know why? Because they have tender flesh and can be eaten alive.*

Once, on a double-dare, Traveler and Willis Tanner had sneaked into the Catholic cathedral on South Temple Street after dark, seeking the graven image of the devil supposed to be hidden there. They hadn't gotten more than a few steps inside when they'd disturbed a roosting bird, whose fluttering wings sent them running for blocks, causing Willis to swear that the devil had changed himself into a bat.

TWENTY-SEVEN

Ida Odegaard was seated on a chrome-trimmed Naugahyde sofa in the hospital's waiting room, reading a Dr. Seuss to the Snarr children, who were crammed as close to her as they could get. At Traveler's approach she stopped reading and looked up, eyes red and swollen, and shook her head to warn him to be careful in front of the children.

The little girl tugged on Ida's sleeve. "More, please, the way Mommy does."

"Your Aunt Ida has to rest for a minute and talk to this man."

"Let me try," the boy said.

"All right, but don't lose my place." She handed him the book. "We'll be right outside."

Traveler followed Mrs. Odegaard across the faded green linoleum and out the door into the oppressive sunlight, where she sat on the narrow step that was all the front entrance the hospital had. Traveler joined her, feeling the sun-scorched concrete through the seat of his jeans.

"I was with Hannah Tempest before she lost consciousness," Ida said without preamble. "Traveler."

"She told you my name?"

"I don't think she meant to at first. For a while there she was out of her head and kept calling me Claire. 'Claire,' she'd say, 'why have you done this to me? He wouldn't have found us if you hadn't made me promise.' Do you know what she meant, Mr. Traveler?"

"I'm not sure you'd believe me if I told you."

Ida shaded her eyes to stare at him. "My husband and I spent most of last night talking. The way we figure it, you and Hannah were lovers, though I would have thought she wasn't your type."

"I'd never met her before coming to Bingham the day before yesterday."

Ida shook her head. "A woman doesn't name her child after a stranger."

"There's no tie between us, blood or otherwise."

"Yet you're here."

Traveler saw no way out except the truth, though he confined it to recounting his turbulent relationship with Claire, her whims, her games, and her determination to give up her child, not his, to Hannah Tempest.

For a long time, Ida stared him in the eye, not speaking, challenging him to flinch, to show any sign of weakness that might reveal him as a liar. When finally she spoke, she sounded weary. "Some of the guilt has to be yours, Mr. Traveler. She was reaching out to you, your Claire, but you didn't help her."

"I didn't know how."

"At least you have a conscience. You wouldn't be here otherwise, would you? Checking up on a child who isn't yours. I think Garth will be comforted to know there's someone around like you in case he takes a turn for the worst."

"What about Hattie's husband?" Traveler said.

"Lyman and young Marty went on life support ten minutes ago and they're about to be called home if you ask me. That's why I fear for Garth's life too."

"Goddammit," Traveler said. He closed his eyes and saw the boy, looking so much like Claire.

■——————■

She knocked on the wooden door frame. "So far, Garth Tempest's fine, but you never know with food poisoning. If I thought he'd agree to it, I'd adopt Angel myself right this minute. Go in there and get his signature on a legal paper. Garth Tempest's not the kind of man to bring up a child alone."

"Angel?"

Her eyes narrowed. "Who do you think we've been talking about."

"Marty. Nicknamed for Moroni."

"Good God, you didn't know, did you? Marty's named for his grandfather, Lyman Martin Snarr. The girl's named for you. Hellsakes, they couldn't call her Moroni, now could they? That would have sounded silly. So they called her Angel."

Traveler felt stunned, though part of him realized that he should have expected Claire to play one last trick. He also felt ashamed of the relief he was feeling that Angel wasn't the one on life support.

"Marty has Claire's coloring," he said.

Ida shrugged. "In case you haven't noticed, Angel has your blue eyes."

"How is she?"

"You saw for yourself when you came in the lobby. Angel and Tommy, the older boy, seemed to have been spared completely."

"Thank God for that."

"How old do you think Hannah Tempest was?" Ida asked him suddenly.

He shook his head.

"You don't have to be diplomatic. She looked like an old woman. I was with her when she died, thinking the same thing myself, that she looked like my own mother when she died, used up. Too much hard work, too many hand-me-down clothes, and a husband who never made enough to keep body and soul together. The fact is, Hannah wasn't much older than you are, Mr. Traveler. A young woman with a lot of life ahead of her."

He nodded, remembering his first impression of Hannah, that she was his mother's age, wearing Kary's kind of house-dress.

"It's terrible to die like that," Ida said, "thinking about what could have been. She was out of her mind, thinking I was Claire, but Hannah's dreams still came through. 'Claire,' she said, 'look at what I have, look at my man. And you let one like that go. I would have traded with you. I would have loved him. I would have borne and raised his children, no matter what. I would never have given them up.' "

Ida blinked, expelling tears. "I didn't realize it then, Mr. Traveler, but Hannah was talking about you. What she said makes some sense now that you've told me about Claire. It makes me sad, too, to know how Hannah felt about the life she had."

He didn't know what to say.

"That's why I'm trusting you. It's also the reason I'll keep quiet about who you really are and tell my husband to do the same."

"Do you know anything else about Garth that I ought to know?"

"He's not the most likable man, but I wouldn't wish what's happened to him on anybody."

"What happens to Angel if he dies?"

"You asking proves I'm right about you, but I don't know and that's a fact. You take my advice and go back to Salt Lake. I'll call you if anything happens to Garth. That's a promise."

A car horn began honking in the distance, one long blast after another.

"That's the signal," she said. "The vote's in early. Kennecott's won. The town will be sold."

TWENTY-EIGHT

The weather broke suddenly. By the time Traveler drove out of the Oquirrh Mountains and into the valley, thunderheads were crossing the Great Salt Lake, pushing a squall front ahead of them. In the thirty minutes it took him to reach the Chester Building, the temperature dropped from eighty-five to fifty. Indian summer had given way to a winterlike runoff that was nearing curb level as he parked on South Temple Street and made a dash for the revolving brass door.

Just inside, Barney Chester stood with his face pressed so close against the plate glass that his breath was fogging his vision. At Traveler's entrance, Chester tore a paper towel from the roll he was holding, wiped a peephole, and said, "For Christ's sake. You ran right by them."

"Church security, you mean? I saw them. Tan, unmarked sedan, two men trying to look inconspicuous, with windshield wipers on intermittent."

"They've been out there spying for the last two days."

Chester rolled off half a dozen paper towels and handed them to Traveler, who mopped his face and blotted his hair.

His shirt was sticking to his back; his running shoes made squishing noises on the lobby's granite floor.

"They're driving me crazy, Moroni. Go out there and talk to them. Find out if they're after me and my building or only waiting around for Mad Bill. Run 'em off if you can. I asked Martin to give me a hand, but he had an appointment at the City and County Building."

"You know they're not going to tell me anything." Traveler held out his hand for more paper towels. "There's something I have to tell my father. Did he say when he'd be back?"

"An hour or so." Chester tossed the roll. "Nephi Bates says we're all under surveillance. He says they follow him everywhere he goes."

"If he's the church spy you've always claimed, he ought to know."

"We're lost. We might as well go into the desert and join Bill and Charlie."

"Don't give up yet. I spoke with a man from the Historical Society while I was in Bingham. He's a great fan of the Chester Building and said he'd look into the story about Thomas Hart Benton."

"I know. Wayne Pinock. He showed up an hour ago with Gussie Gustavson's son in tow. Nephi's upstairs right now giving them the tour."

Traveler ran off the last of the paper towels and began mopping up the puddle at his feet.

"You should have been here when they arrived," Chester said. "Gussie Junior gave me quite a start. He looks just like his father at that age. Fifty-two Gussie was when he died. I'd known him for twenty years by then. After that, Junior never set foot in this building again, not until today. The moment he did, you know what he said? 'I don't care what you call this place, to me it will always be the Gustavson Building.' Like father, like son. Gussie was just as ornery and would have said the same thing."

Traveler balled up the soggy towels and carried them to the wastebasket behind the cigar counter.

Barney followed. "There's mulled coffee to take the chill off."

"I'd better go up to the office and change first."

As Traveler was about to ring for the elevator, the cables hummed and the grillwork cage descended slowly. At ground level, Nephi Bates opened the brass door to emit Wayne Pinock, who was carrying an aluminum equipment case, and a middle-aged man whose dark blue suit looked freshly pressed, his shoes so highly polished they could have been patent leather.

"Gussie, this is Moroni Traveler," Chester said.

"Gustav Gustavson," the man corrected. He didn't offer to shake hands, so Traveler ignored him and reintroduced himself to Pinock, who raised an eyebrow behind Gustavson's back before stowing his case next to the cigar stand.

Gustavson's appearance, despite Chester's claim, didn't match the old photos of Gussie Senior, who'd been bald, with only a fringe around the ears, while Junior's hair was as precise as his clothes. Traveler moved closer. The hair was too precise, he decided.

Gustavson noticed Traveler's stare, started to reach for his scalp, caught himself, and backed up a step.

Intending to convey sympathy, Traveler smiled.

Gustavson misinterpreted. "Having a handicap isn't funny, Mr. Traveler. I still remember the day when a bishop came to our Sunday School and told us that Catholics never go bald. 'They're all in league with the devil,' he said, 'and need hair to cover their horns.' When I started to lose mine, I left the Saints for the Pope, but it didn't do any good. I still went bald, just like my father. It was all the inheritance he left me, though he always said this building should have been mine, that it was stolen from me."

"I heard he lost it to Barney gambling."

"Gambling debts aren't legal, my father said."

"This should all go on tape," Pinock put in, "not for legal reasons, you understand, but for an oral history to go along with the photographs I intend to take."

———•———

165

"You already have my father's photo collection," Gustavson said.

"Technically," Pinock said, making it obvious he was speaking for Traveler's benefit, "those photos are still your property. According to our records, they were only loaned to the Historical Society."

"My father took them himself when they were building this place. That was before I was born."

"Can you remember what he told you about those days?" Traveler said.

"Like what?" Gustavson sounded belligerent.

"Who painted the murals, for instance."

Gustavson studied the ceiling for a moment. "My father was shrewd there. I remember him telling me that he made a deal to get the government to pay most of the costs."

"That was the WPA at its best," Pinock said.

"Amen," Nephi Bates added.

Gustavson stepped over to the cigar stand, where the eternal flame was flickering badly, leaned against the counter, and craned his neck to examine the ceiling from a different angle. "My father said the mural was a religious experience for him, but I don't see it. I don't see much of anything but soot. You wouldn't recognize Brigham Young if it wasn't for the wagon train."

"Me and Nephi are going to start cleaning the ceiling tomorrow," Chester said.

"I'll want before-and-after shots," Pinock said.

"Father said God looked down on him from that ceiling," Gustavson went on. "For years I've been driving past this building, knowing that if God was looking down on anybody, it should be me."

He moved away from the counter to run his hands over one of the massive Doric columns that held up the ceiling. "These are made of temple marble, my father used to tell me, the same kind they laid down across the street." He spread his arms. "This was my bedtime story, the one he told every night. About my lost legacy."

166

Gustavson shook his head. "My father had no right to bet my future on a game of cards." He left the column to confront Chester at close range. "You had no right to accept the bet."

"It wasn't just one bet. Your father owed me a lot of money. The Chester Building was the only way he could get out from under, he told me finally, insisting that I accept it as collateral, as one last double-or-nothing bet."

Gustavson smiled crookedly. "Count on it, Chester. I'll be here the day demolition starts. It's going to do my soul good to see this place come down around your ears. After that, I'll be able to pass by here in peace. You can forget the photos, too."

He turned away from Chester to point a finger at Pinock. "I want them back from the Historical Society. From now on, no one gets to see them but me."

Waving off any attempted argument, Gustavson tossed change on the cigar counter, grabbed a copy of the morning *Tribune*, which he spread over his toupee, and walked out into the rain.

"That's why we take our own photographs whenever we can," Pinock said, shaking his head. "History should be shared, not left to the whims of those who inherit it. Thank God I'm in time to preserve this piece of our heritage."

"I should have been nicer to him," Chester said.

"I've already been over the photographs," Pinock said. "I didn't see any that would help you, but I did make some copies of the artwork. It's a good thing, too. My experience is that old photos seldom survive if they're not on file with us."

He moved to the center of the lobby, knelt down to feel the floor, then spread out on his back so he could stare up at the ceiling. "Can we get any more light in here?"

At a nod from Chester, Nephi Bates opened a recessed panel in the wall near the men's room and began throwing switches. The art deco chandeliers, designed to cast a golden glow, not candlepower, intensified the shadows at the corners of the ceiling.

Pinock sat up, groaned loudly, and got to his feet to retrieve a battery-powered lantern from his equipment case. Caught in the bright beam, Brigham Young's image came alive at the head of his pioneer wagon train. The artist, whoever he was, had captured a feeling of raw power. The Brigham Young portrayed there was more than a man; he was God's chosen prophet.

"I'm no art expert," Pinock said, "but that could be Thomas Hart Benton, all right. He had a lot of imitators, though, but whoever did this was no amateur."

For the next few minutes he swept the beam of light back and forth across the ceiling, looking for a signature.

"The nicotine and smoke buildup is pretty bad," he said finally. "There's always a chance, though, that you'll find signatures when you clean the mural."

"I'll get scaffolding in here tomorrow," Chester said.

"If you find Benton's name, you can raise some hell, and maybe even some extra money before they tear this place down. One thing's certain, though. There's no chance of saving that ceiling separately from the rest of the building, not the way the Chester's built."

Pinock walked back and forth across the lobby several times, his gaze never leaving the ceiling, before coming to a stop in front of the cigar stand, where he picked up one of the cups of coffee Chester had set out on the counter. He took a sip and smacked his lips. "When the rain lets up, I'll go out to the van and bring in some portable lights so I can start shooting. When you get the scaffolding up tomorrow, I'd like to use it for my close-ups if you don't mind."

Nephi Bates stepped forward. "I'd be honored to help you."

The comment brought a sigh from Chester. "Why not? I want people to remember this place when we're all gone."

Traveler shivered.

"You'd better get out of those wet clothes, Mo." Chester slipped behind the counter to fetch the jug wine he kept stashed out of sight, topped off one of the Styrofoam cups, and pushed it toward Traveler. "Is anyone else in need of medicinal comfort?"

Pinock accepted the offer while Bates, his pinched face condemning those who flouted the Word of Wisdom, retreated to his elevator.

Before Traveler could finish his coffee, the revolving door whooshed into action and Charlie Redwine, wearing one of Bill's flowing robes, came hurtling into the lobby. His hair was matted, the robe filthy despite the rain; he looked on the verge of collapse as he staggered toward the cigar stand. The two plainclothesmen from the tan sedan—both big men, one a Tongan like those the church recruited for the BYU football team—were right behind him.

"Sanctuary," Charlie croaked.

Chester poured straight wine into a cup but Charlie waved away the offer and whispered, "Water."

Chester called over Nephi Bates, who didn't look happy at the summons but still accepted an empty cup to fill in the men's room. When he returned, Charlie drank it all before collapsing onto the floor, where he sat cross-legged. "At the prophet's bidding, I've crossed the desert without water. I have passed God's fiery test."

One of the security men, the Tongan, took a cellular phone from beneath his raincoat and punched in numbers. "The Sandwich Man has arrived."

Because of the robe, he'd obviously mistaken Charlie for Mad Bill.

"He's an Indian," Bates told the man. "Not the Sandwich Prophet."

The man relayed the information into the phone. After a moment he said, "I understand," disconnected, and glared at Charlie. "I expect a warrant for your arrest to arrive within the hour." With that, he and his companion left the building.

"The prophet and I have survived God's crucible," Charlie said.

"Where is Bill?" Traveler asked.

"He sent me ahead to prepare the way for him. 'Tell them,' he said, 'that God's fire has burned away our sins and purified our hearts. God has revealed himself. He has shown us the way.' "

Traveler moved in for a closer look, checking Charlie's breath and eyes to see if he had been drinking. There was no sign of alcohol, though his peyote pouch was empty.

"When can we expect Bill to arrive?"

"Before I am martyred," Charlie said, "and in time to found his monument."

TWENTY-NINE

Traveler fetched one of Bill's dry robes from the basement of the Chester Building before accompanying Charlie upstairs to the office. While the Indian changed clothes, Traveler stared out at the temple, whose granite had taken on an obsidian luster in the rain. The Angel Moroni was lost in low cloud. Traveler felt lost too, more so now that he'd found Moroni Traveler the Third, whose life, like his, seemed linked to one of Claire's whims.

The temple lights came on, well ahead of dusk because of the darkness of the afternoon. The sudden illumination caused Charlie's reflection to intrude on Traveler's view.

"You've made a remarkable recovery if you walked all the way from Bob's Big Indian," Traveler said.

The Indian settled onto the client chair in front of Martin's desk. "God showed me the way."

Traveler raised a fist, thumb extended, as if he were hitchhiking.

"God's hand was at work, not mine. We are resurrected, Bill and I."

Sighing, Traveler left the window to change into fresh jeans, a Black Watch tartan flannel shirt over a white turtleneck, and well-worn running shoes.

"It's dark enough to be dinnertime," Charlie said.

"Does that mean you're hungry?"

Before the Indian could answer, the phone rang.

Traveler handed Charlie eating money as he picked up the phone. "Moroni Traveler and Son."

"This is Ida Odegaard, Mr. Traveler. I promised I'd call even if the news was bad. Lyman Snarr slipped into a coma and passed away an hour ago. The boy, Marty, joined him in heaven not five minutes ago." Her sigh sounded like static on the line.

"And Garth Tempest?"

"He's a lucky man, the doctors say. They just released him from the hospital. That's one child, at least, who won't be an orphan."

"Is Angel all right?"

"She's fine, and so far no one else has come down sick either. We've had doctors in from Salt Lake, and even they can't agree what caused the sickness, though they're sure it was some kind of food poisoning. Until we know for certain, the rumors will keep flying up and down Bingham Canyon, though you'll never convince me that it was deliberate, like so many people are saying."

"Did they eat anything the rest of us didn't?"

"Didn't I say? They think whatever it was, was in the lemonade, so it really is a miracle that Angel and Tommy escaped."

Traveler closed his eyes and saw the picnic table again, cups full of lemonade standing around the thermos. The women were drinking it, so was Snarr, while he and Martin stuck to beer. The children, he remembered, had fled to the neighboring table, lured there by Ida Odegaard's chocolate cake. His memory showed them drinking milk.

"I've never heard of lemonade going bad," he said.

"Practically everybody in town made lemonade. The lemons

all came from the same place, too. That's why they're checking the water at the Tempest house now."

"Who's checking?"

"The sheriff's men."

"What about Garth," Traveler said, "is he well enough to take care of Angel?"

"Don't you worry about that, Mr. Traveler. Angel is staying with us for the time being, until Garth gets back on his feet. Now, before you ask any more questions, my husband is standing right here and wants to talk to you."

"Traveler," Almon Odegaard said abruptly, "I don't like people coming here pretending they're somebody else."

"I had to protect the girl."

"I find it hard to believe that she was named after you as a joke. If you're lying about that, if you're the child's real father, God knows what else you've done. I told the sheriff's investigator the same thing, so you can expect a call from him. Jesse Snarr knows you've been playing games too. Doctors are supposed to be objective, but he lost both parents and a brother, so I'd watch out for him if I were you."

"What does he think about the food poisoning?"

"He's like me. I want to hear you tell your story to my face before I'll believe it." Odegaard hung up.

Traveler started to dial the sheriff's office, then had second thoughts.

"When my father gets back," he told Charlie, "tell him I've gone back to Bingham."

"I'll send out for Chinese. That way I won't have to leave the office."

"Save something for Bill."

Charlie eyed the twenty-dollar bill that Traveler had given him.

Shaking his head, Traveler handed over another twenty before leaving the office. When Nephi Bates let him off in the lobby, Martin was standing in front of the elevator, waiting to go up.

———

173

Traveler shepherded him over to the cigar stand, out of Bates's earshot, where Barney Chester was disassembling the eternal flame again.

"Do you think I ought to ban smoking in here?" Chester said. "After we get the ceiling cleaned, I mean."

"Why don't you check out front and see how church security's doing?" Traveler said.

Chester put down the flame spout he was holding and wiped his oily hands. "A few minutes of privacy coming up. Call me when you're through."

Once Chester was gone, Traveler relayed the news from the Odegaards. The moment he finished, Martin said, "Christ, I was carrying that little boy on my shoulder at the picnic." He touched Traveler's shoulder.

"Mrs. Odegaard assures me that Angel's going to be fine," Traveler said.

"She doesn't look like Claire."

"Claire told me she was blond as a child."

"You drank some of that lemonade, didn't you?" Martin asked.

Traveler shook his head. "After the football game, we were both drinking beer, don't you remember?"

"I don't like it," Martin said. "Only the people sitting at one particular picnic table got sick. That makes me wonder if it wasn't deliberate."

"In that case, who hated the Tempests and the Snarrs enough to do it?"

"We could have been among the dead."

Traveler nodded. "I'm on my way back to Bingham right now."

"To keep an eye on Angel, I hope."

"Among other things, like calming down the mayor. Do you want to come with me?"

"Not just yet," Martin said. "I've come up with something interesting on the Chester Building. With one exception, the lots surrounding the building are owned by a single holding company, probably the church, though I won't know for sure until I do more research."

"The city wouldn't be crazy enough to try condemning church property."

"You may be right, but one thing's for sure. Your old friend, Josiah Ellsworth, the White Prophet, is listed on the holding company's board of directors. Sam Howe's name was there, too, as attorney of record."

"Who owns the other piece of property you mentioned, the exception?"

"Apparently you do. Your name's on the deed. You'll be a rich man when this block is developed."

"What the hell is going on?"

"Maybe it's meant to be a bribe. I'm sure we'll find out soon enough."

"There must be a signature somewhere, one that's supposed to be mine," Traveler said.

"I can't check that until tomorrow. That's one of the reasons I'd better stay here in town, so you watch your back out there in Bingham."

THIRTY

Traveler didn't reach Bingham Canyon until after dark. By then, the rain had slacked off to a fine drizzle. The air smelled fresh, with only a trace of Kennecott to compete with the mountain sage. No lights showed in Emma Dugan's boardinghouse and no one answered his knock, so he left the Jeep parked out front and walked up Main Street to the hospital, only to find the door locked and a posted notice giving a telephone number to call in case of emergency.

After backtracking to the Pastime Bar, a round of drinks got him Shaky Johnson's personal escort to the mayor's house, a narrow two-story clapboard that fronted Main Street like most everything else in town. Johnson stopped short of the porch. "The mayor told me to keep an eye out for you, so tell him I did my duty. I delivered you just like he wanted."

He started to turn away but changed his mind. "Miz Odegaard's not one to turn people away, but if you end up needing a place to stay tonight, we can always put you up at the Pastime." He tipped his cap and walked away.

Traveler watched the man out of sight before knocking on

the door. The porch light, a yellow bug bulb, came on. A curtain moved at the window next to the door. A moment later Mayor Almon Odegaard, holding a revolver at his side, its muzzle pointed at the ground, opened the door, looked Traveler up and down, and finally beckoned him inside.

Once across the threshold, Traveler held his arms out as if expecting to be searched.

"That's not necessary." Odegaard went up on tiptoe to stow the revolver on top of a six-foot china cabinet next to the living room's front window. The room also held an old-fashioned rocking chair and a narrow sofa and matching armchair that reminded Traveler of pictures from a Sears catalog.

"The children are in the kitchen," Odegaard said. "So's Garth Tempest. Be careful what you say around him."

"Does he know my real name?"

"We haven't told him yet."

Traveler started for the kitchen but Odegaard held him back.

"I want to hear what you have to say for yourself first," Odegaard said. "About you and this woman, Angel's real mother."

Keeping his voice down, Traveler did his best to explain his on-and-off relationship with Claire. When he finished, Odegaard shook his head. "I don't think you'd make up something like that. Now what about Hannah Tempest?"

"I never met her before coming to Bingham. I swear it."

Odegaard took a deep breath. "I don't like what's going on here, but I'll believe you until you're proved wrong. Now let's get in the kitchen before Garth comes looking for us."

The kitchen was the same size as the living room, maybe twelve by twelve, but warmer because of a steaming pot of soup bubbling on the stove. In the center of the room was a battered oak dining table, around which sat Tommy Snarr, Angel and her father, Garth Tempest, and Ida Odegaard. The children looked unchanged, but Tempest was no longer the vigorous man who'd opposed Traveler at the football game.

His head hung loosely, as if his neck muscles had gone slack; his shoulders slumped; his staring eyes showed no recognition when Traveler nodded at him.

"Father," Mrs. Odegaard told her husband, "you fetch another chair."

"I think it's time the children went to bed," he said.

She looked from her husband's face to Traveler's before nodding, rising to her feet, and holding her hands out. Tommy obeyed her summons immediately, but Angel slid off her chair and tried to climb onto Tempest's lap. His only response was to stare at his folded hands which lay on the blue-and-white checkered tablecloth.

"Come to me, Angel," Ida said. "Your father's tired."

"I want a good-night kiss," the girl said.

Tempest made no move until Odegaard tapped him on the shoulder. Only then did he lean down to Angel's level. She threw her arms around his neck and kissed his unshaven cheek. He didn't look at her.

As soon as the children had gone upstairs with Ida, Traveler sat opposite Tempest while Odegaard, unasked, filled a bowl with soup and set it in front of Traveler.

"What about you, Garth?" Odegaard said. "It's time we got some hot food in you."

Still staring down at his hands, Tempest shook his head. "The cramps have let up some, but my gut still feels like it's on fire." He'd spoken slowly, with a pause to catch his breath in the middle of the sentence.

"Have they found out what made you sick?" Traveler asked.

Tempest raised his head. "This town's full of poison. The mines have been polluting us for years, so it's no wonder the water's unsafe."

"No one else got sick," the mayor pointed out.

"I don't care what you say, the company's to blame. There's no one else."

The mayor shook his head. "They were still using outhouses when I was a boy, some of them draining right into the creek beds. But there was never any disease, not even cholera in the old days. You know why? The runoff from the mines killed all the bacteria."

Tempest said, "We didn't get a chance to vote, me and my family, so the election isn't legal."

"It wouldn't make any difference, Garth. We lost by more than four votes. Otherwise, I'd ask for a new election myself."

"They didn't know they'd win in advance. We all thought it would be a close one. You said so yourself. You said we all had to get out and vote. You said one yes or no could make the difference."

"I wanted to believe it, Garth, but . . ." The mayor spread his hands.

"Refresh my memory," Traveler said. "Who led the fight to sell the town, besides the company?"

"You played football with them," the mayor answered. "Father Bannon and Frank Murdock. Murdock owns a lot of shanties in this town. From what I hear, the company offered him a lot more than they're worth. God knows what they offered for Father Bannon's church."

"He wouldn't get the money."

"He's always wanted a big church in a big city."

Tempest rose abruptly, his arms crossed over his stomach. "I'd better go. The cramps are starting to act up again."

"You're welcome to stay here," the mayor said.

"You've done enough already, taking care of Angel. Besides, when I'm sick I want my own bed."

"I'll see you home if Mr. Traveler doesn't mind."

"I was about to leave anyway," Traveler said.

"You'll have to answer to my wife if you don't finish your soup." Odegaard retrieved his revolver on the way out.

Traveler was about to follow them when Mrs. Odegaard returned to the kitchen, sat opposite him, and supervised his every spoonful.

"I don't know what's going to become of the children," she said when he'd finished eating. "Right now, they don't quite understand what's happened to them. When I think back to my own parents, how important they were to me and how much I loved them, I don't know what I would have done if I'd lost them at such an early age. It makes me want to—" Abruptly, she stopped speaking and stared beyond Traveler.

He turned around to see Angel standing in the doorway, clutching a ragged doll and looking frightened.

"It's all right, dear. Come to Aunt Ida."

The girl stopped next to Traveler and looked up at him, blinking. "Daddy says Mommy isn't coming home anymore."

Traveler looked to Ida, who sighed deeply and said, "It's God's will, honey."

"Mommy doesn't love me."

"She loves you more than you'll ever know," Traveler said.

"Daddy doesn't love me."

"Of course he does," Ida said.

Angel shook her head. "He told me so." She handed her doll to Traveler. "Mommy said you were a nice man, so you can take care of Dolly. She's all alone now."

Traveler accepted the offering but didn't know what to say.

"She wants you to hold her," Ida said as if sensing Traveler's uncertainty.

Traveler offered a hand, which Angel used to pull herself onto his lap. She took back the doll and held it in her arms just as Traveler was holding her in his. He rocked them both while Ida sang.

> "The other night I had a dream,
> I dreamt that I had died;
> I flapped my wings like an eagle,
> And flew into the skies.
> And there I saw Moroni,
> A-sitting on a spire;
> He asked me up and said we'd sup
> On this most humble fare:
> Oh—carrot greens,
> Good old carrot greens,
> Cornbread and buttermilk
> And good old carrot greens."

Angel's eyelids closed. Neither Traveler nor Ida spoke for a long time. Finally, Ida whispered, "If you don't mind sleeping on the screen porch, you're welcome to stay the night with us."

"It will be easier if I go back to Emma Dugan's boardinghouse."

"Emma left this afternoon, I'm afraid. She said there was no sense sticking around to see the place die. She left the key with a neighbor so the movers can come next week and take everything away. Besides, you can't leave now. You'll wake Angel."

Ida's smile seemed to say she didn't want to be left alone either, at least not until her husband returned.

Angel whimpered in her sleep.

"I hate to say this," Ida said softly, "but I wish I could keep Angel for myself. Did you hear her, Mr. Traveler? Did you hear what her father said to her?"

"She may have misunderstood."

"Don't you believe it. Even if children don't understand what's being said, they can sense things." She laid a hand on her breast. "Inside, I know that child needs someone to love her now. I wish it could be me, but Almon and I are going to live with our daughter and her husband up in Heber Valley. That's the most beautiful place on earth, Mr. Traveler, and the best place I can think of to raise a child like Angel, but . . ."

"Have you suggested adoption to Garth Tempest?"

"At our time of life Almon doesn't think we can afford it. Our daughter has young children of her own to worry about. Besides, we're not about to ask a man like Garth Tempest for favors."

Traveler's arm grew numb. When he tried to shift Angel's position she whimpered again.

"Do you remember when you were a child, Mr. Traveler, when you were sick and your mother would make you feel better by just touching your brow?"

"It was my father who had the magic touch."

Ida looked at the little girl and shook her head.

"What kind of a man is Garth Tempest?" he said.

"You'll have to talk to my husband about that. Now, if

you'll excuse me, I'll go make up the bed on the screen porch for you."

By the time the mayor returned, Traveler, with Ida's help, had tucked Angel beneath the down comforter that covered the sofa.

"There's whiskey in the kitchen, Mr. Traveler," Ida said. "We keep it for medicinal purposes normally, but this is one time we're all in need of a stimulant. You and Almon go on in and get to know each other better. I'll stay here for a while and make sure the child settles down."

As the men left the room Ida began singing. For a moment Traveler thought it was "Oh, Susannah," then realized it was the same "Handcart Song" that Martin had once used as a lullaby.

In the kitchen, with the door closed behind them, Odegaard said, "I hope my wife hasn't been telling tales."

"She insisted that you were the one to tell me about Garth Tempest."

Odegaard went up on tiptoe to snare a whiskey bottle from the top shelf over the sink. From an adjacent cupboard he took jelly glasses and set them on the table.

"If you want to lighten your sin," he said, smiling, "you'll have to use water. Say when."

Traveler stopped him at half a glass. Odegaard followed suit. Neither of them added water.

"We discussed adoption," Odegaard said. "Did Ida tell you that?"

Traveler nodded.

"In the end personal considerations made the decision for us, and that's probably for the best, because I don't know how Garth would take to such a proposal."

"I could talk to him," Traveler said.

"On whose behalf?"

Traveler was still thinking that over when Odegaard continued. "Do you know what they call him? Temper Tempest. He got that nickname when he worked the mine, though he's never shown that side to me. My wife, though, she claims clairvoyance at times, and she says he gives off bad vibrations. She says he's a violent man."

"What do you think?" Traveler asked.

The mayor toyed with his glass for a moment. "Hannah never looked at another man, not around Garth. The men around here knew better than to let him catch them looking at her, that's for sure."

The kitchen door opened far enough for Ida to show herself without actually entering the room. Obviously, she'd been listening. "Stop beating around the bush, Almon, and say it right out."

"Now Ida."

"I fear for the child, Mr. Traveler. We both do."

"He's never hit her," Odegaard said. "Those houses down on Hagland Alley are so close together the neighbors would know if he had."

Ida pushed through the swinging door and into the kitchen. "Those so-called neighbors never did anything about Hannah's black eyes."

"Things happen between a husband and wife."

Ida flicked her wrist, dismissing the comment. "Hannah tried to leave him once, but ended up coming back. If she'd stayed away, she'd be alive now."

Odegaard reached for his drink but Ida beat him to it. She sipped, made a face, and added water from the tap before handing it back to her husband.

"Ida's right. Hannah, God rest her, tried to get away. She went to live with her sister Hattie. We didn't know them back then, but Ida heard about it from Hattie, who said Hannah only went back to Garth because of the child."

"I've seen too many people try to stick together for the sake of the children," Ida said. "The children always get hurt. That's why I worry about Angel. Maybe I don't know the whole truth about why she's named for you, Mr. Traveler, but if you ask me, you're her only hope."

THIRTY-ONE

A distant whistle, probably something to do with Kennecott, woke Traveler the next morning. Smelling coffee, he rose from the bed though it was still dark, donned yesterday's clothes, and went into the kitchen where Ida was setting the table. The warmth from the open oven made him realize how cold the screen porch had been.

"We keep Postum if you'd rather have it."

"I could use the caffeine," he said, answering her unspoken question as to whether he followed the church's Word of Wisdom.

She filled two mugs from an old-fashioned metal coffeepot and handed him one. He was about to drink when another whistle blew, this one sounding a long time.

"Hold on to to your hat," she said. "Kennecott's blasting early today."

Traveler heard the rumble first, a moment before the house shook violently. Dust, erupting from every joint and joist, immediately filled the air. Somewhere outside, power lines arced, charging the kitchen with an eerie blue light that brought the dust motes to life.

Holding his breath, Traveler went to the back door and opened it, half expecting to see the landscape littered with collapsed buildings. But a heavy mist, barely shy of rain, shrouded most of Bingham Canyon.

Ida touched his shoulder.

"They have steam shovels that scoop up fifteen tons of ore at one time," she said. "They'll gobble this whole place up before you know it. Soon, there won't be anything left to show we were ever here."

She edged past him, still holding her coffee mug, and led the way around the side of the house. Out front, half a dozen pickup trucks lined Main Street, where people were already loading their life's belongings.

Hugging herself, Ida said, "Half the town will be abandoned by this evening. A week from now there won't be anybody here. You'd think Kennecott could have waited until we're gone."

"I was planning to talk to someone from the company."

"It's too big," she said. "They pass you from one to the other. The buck never stops and no one's accountable. Besides, why would you want to bother now that everything is decided?"

"When people die someone should be held accountable."

"Don't go believing rumors now, or Garth Tempest either. Something got into the lemonade by accident, that's all. An act of God. Anyway, the election was only a formality. The company was never threatened."

"I'd like to hear that from them."

"The man to see, if you can get to him, is Oren Lathrop. He's overseeing the expansion of the mine. He's not one of these lawyer types either. He started in the smelter and worked his way up."

From inside the house came the sound of Angel's wailing.

Ida shook her head. "I don't know if you heard her, but she kept waking up with nightmares. Finally I had to take her into bed with me."

Oren Lathrop's office was a portable metal shed overlooking the world's largest open-pit copper mine. It was featured on postcards and admired daily by hundreds of bus-borne tourists. A man-made wonder of the world, Kennecott called it. Seen from the shed's small casement window, the mine reminded Traveler of a canker eating away at the Oquirrh Mountains.

"You have that look," Lathrop said. "A missionary who wants to save the trees or the whales, or some such thing."

"I don't like seeing things die."

Lathrop smiled as if to say he'd guessed right. "Sit down and convert me, Mr. Traveler."

Traveler opened a folding metal chair that had been leaning against the corrugated wall and set it up facing Lathrop's makeshift desk, a sheet of plywood resting on sawhorses. Blueprints and papers covered the entire wooden surface.

"I was surprised that you agreed to see me so quickly," Traveler said.

"In this state it's always wise to give priority to someone named Moroni."

Lathrop's smile deepened the creases in his leathery face. He took off his hard hat, with its Kennecott logo, and ran a hand over his matted gray hair. Safety goggles dangled around his neck from an elastic cord. His tan workshirt was sweat-stained and rumpled.

Traveler handed him a business card but Lathrop waved it away.

"I know who you are, Mr. Traveler. A private detective from the big city, obviously here to investigate the deaths in Bingham Canyon."

"Only a few locals know who I am."

"The church isn't the only one with security people working for it," Lathrop said. "I'll save you some time. The election was window dressing, nothing more. In this state the law gives mining companies the right of eminent domain. We can take what we need, Mr. Traveler. We don't have to kill people, despite the rumors you've heard in town. We only held the election to keep the bad publicity to a minimum."

"From what I hear the dead would have voted against you."

"You know the count wasn't that close."

"There's talk that poison from the mine, maybe some kind of runoff, got into the water system."

"If that had happened, the whole town would have been affected." Lathrop pushed a folder across the desktop. "Take a look for yourself. The water's been tested and we got a clean bill of health from the authorities."

Traveler glanced through the file. "Let me be more personal, then. Did you know the Tempests or the Snarrs?"

"To say hello to."

"Did they have any enemies as far as you know?"

"Other than us, you mean?" Lathrop shook his head. "I have no idea."

"I don't see how the poisoning could have been an accident."

"Even if I agree with you, it has nothing to do with the company."

"They're saying Father Jake Bannon and Frank Murdock work for you," Traveler said. "Maybe they got overzealous."

"Their motives are their own, I assure you. Just as yours are, Mr. Traveler."

The smug look on Lathrop's face said he knew more about Traveler than company security, no matter how good, should have been able to provide on short notice.

"The town's going to be a ghost in a few days, Mr. Traveler. People will be looking for new jobs; they'll end up scattered all over the state. Friends and neighbors may never see one another again. As for us, we'll start demolishing the town as soon as it's vacated, to make way for expansion of the mine. City hall, the hospital, the stores along Main Street, everything has to go. So take my advice. If you want to talk to anybody else—Dr. Snarr, for instance—you'd better get going. Who knows? The man might have some important information."

Traveler stood up. "I have the feeling you could save me the trouble."

"You're the detective, Mr. Traveler, not me."

THIRTY-TWO

Traveler found Jesse Snarr lying on the sofa in the hospital lobby, his unshaven face grimacing even in sleep. Traveler was about to wake him when Snarr twitched violently and sat up, wide-eyed and staring.

"Jesus," he sighed. "For a second there, when I sensed you standing over me, I thought you were my father. I thought he'd come to fetch me home for dinner. I thought it was all a nightmare and that everything was back to normal."

He walked away from Traveler, stopping in front of the glass door that fronted Main Street. As soon as Traveler joined him Snarr said, "Look out there, will you?" He rapped a knuckle against the plate glass. "Most of those shacks and cabins should have been condemned years ago. Why people stayed here and lived in them I don't know. I'll be glad when there's nothing left but an open-pit mine."

Traveler wanted to comfort him but didn't know how. All he could say was, "I'm here as a private investigator."

Snarr leaned his head against the glass. "I'm not one to listen to gossip. I don't believe for a minute that the company is responsible for what happened to my family. But someone is."

"Do you think it was deliberate, then?"

"Let's cut the crap. I know that Angel was named after you, but that doesn't tell me your interest in her or my sister-in-law."

Traveler gave him a business card.

"It says 'Moroni Traveler and *Son,*'" Snarr said.

"My father's named Moroni too."

"And Angel?"

Traveler hesitated.

"I'm not about to tell Garth anything unless I have to."

As briefly as possible, Traveler explained his relationship with Claire, and her arrangement with Hannah Tempest.

"If the girl's not yours," Snarr said finally, "why are you here?"

"My father wants a grandchild, even by proxy."

"My mother used to say the same thing to me. 'It's time you got married and raised children of your own. It's time you gave me grandchildren.' Now, I'll be raising Tommy instead. That's a blood obligation, Mr. Traveler. Your motive I don't understand."

Traveler thought about his relationship with Martin, a father without blood obligation who was much closer to him because they lacked a genetic tie. He settled for saying, "I owe Claire."

"How much?"

"That depends on what you tell me about the poison."

Snarr took a deep breath and let it out slowly. "I'll tell you what I told the sheriff. Aunt Hannah made the lemonade. Because of that, I personally searched her house from top to bottom, every drawer, every cupboard. There wasn't anything lethal that could have gotten into the drink by mistake, at least nothing that wouldn't have tasted so bad that no one would have drunk it.

"I talked to everybody who was sitting nearby at the picnic, too. From what I've been able to learn, the more lemonade my family drank, the worse their chances of surviving. Garth is only alive because he switched to beer. As to what actually killed them, I won't know until I hear back from Salt Lake on the tissue, urine, and blood samples I sent for analysis. If it turns out to be poison, God help whoever did it."

"Your responsibility is to Tommy," Traveler said.

"You weren't there when my parents and my brother died. You didn't see their suffering. Diarrhea, chills, nosebleeds, vomiting, and I couldn't do a thing. I was helpless."

"What kind of poison causes symptoms like that?"

"Whatever it was, it attacked the liver, I know that much. Which means Garth could still have trouble sometime down the road. He'll have to monitor himself carefully from now on, and there's always the possibility he may need a transplant one day."

Snarr stared at Traveler so hard the skin quivered around his eyes. "Now that I think about it, you were sitting with my parents at the picnic."

"I stuck to the beer."

"Christ!" Snarr said. "My mother didn't believe a woman should drink beer in public."

Shaking his head, Snarr returned to the sofa, where he sat leaning forward, his arms resting on his thighs. "Lyman Snarr adopted me as his own when my real father died. Every spare nickel went to get me through those first four years of college, until I got a scholarship for medical school. I didn't know it until later, but he had to take a part-time job as bartender down at the White Elephant Saloon to do it. He was going to keep it up, too, taking extra jobs to get Tommy and Marty through college.

"We'll be drinking to Lyman's memory tomorrow at a farewell party down at the White Elephant, which will be open one last time with me behind the bar. I've invited all our friends. You're welcome to come too, Traveler."

Snarr clenched his fists so hard his arms trembled. "Don't worry. I'll check the seals on the bottles myself, to make sure no one else dies."

THIRTY-THREE

Traveler used the pay phone in the hospital lobby to call his father. Once assured that Angel was still in good hands, Martin calmed down enough to listen to the rest of Traveler's report.

"What do your instincts tell you?" Martin asked when Traveler finished.

"To keep looking."

Martin sighed. "I've been doing some looking of my own. Remember that lot someone put in your name? Well, you have the church to thank for it."

"Have you been smoking Charlie's tobacco?"

"Your mother was right," Martin said. "Naming you for an angel was a revelation from God. 'God takes care of his Moronis,' she said. 'My angel, my Moroni, will have someone to watch over him. Someone with power and money.' "

"You said she named me after you. Her way of keeping you around after she'd been unfaithful."

Martin snorted. "I traced the deeds and bills of sale on parcels in the Chester Building's block. Your parcel was purchased by the Etinad Investment Group, then transferred over to you."

"I thought you said it was the church."

"Do you have a pen?" Martin said.

"I don't have any paper to write on."

"Use your hand."

Traveler decided to use the wall, which was already covered with phone numbers and graffiti.

"Mark down Etinad," Martin said. "E-T-I-N-A-D. Have you got it?"

"Yes."

"Spell it to me backward."

"D-A-N-I-T-E."

"That's right. The Danites, the Sons of Dan, the church's avenging angels. And guess who's CEO."

"Josiah Ellsworth," Traveler said.

"It makes you think, doesn't it?"

"Are you saying my mother knew him?"

"Like I said before, Kary always claimed to have friends in high places."

"Did she know Ellsworth or not?"

"It could be a setup," Martin said. "A way of giving you a financial reason to keep your mouth shut about the Chester Building. Of course, since the property's already in your name, I can't see what leverage they'd have."

"So we're back to friends in high places," Traveler said.

"Someone loves you, that's for sure. Someone's trying to make you rich."

Traveler tried to visualize Josiah Ellsworth as he'd seen him on the temple grounds. A tall man certainly, Traveler's height, though much lighter in build. Then again, Ellsworth had never had occasion to bulk up to play football.

"I'd guess Ellsworth to be your age," Traveler said.

Martin chuckled. "He's more your size, too, if that's what you're thinking"

"Does he have children?"

"If a man wants to leave a legacy for his children, property's always good."

Traveler held his breath, wondering if Martin was on the verge of revelation.

After a few seconds of silence, Martin said, "Charlie's here in the office. He's on the other line and wants to speak with you."

"Bill's coming has been announced," Charlie said immediately.

Martin interpreted. "Bill will leave the desert and reach the Chester Building at sunset. They'd both like you here for the ceremony."

Charlie grunted.

"So would I," Martin said. "In any case, there's not much more you can do there until the medical report verifies the cause of death. Just make sure someone watches what Angel eats."

"I'll stop by the Odegaards on my way out of town," Traveler said.

"Give her Bill's blessing," Charlie said. "Mine too."

THIRTY-FOUR

The last of the storm clouds were passing to the east over the Wasatch Mountains by the time Traveler reached the Chester Building. With sunset only minutes away, Charlie, Nephi Bates, and Barney Chester were already gathered on the sidewalk. Charlie, who'd forsaken jeans and checkered shirt for ceremonial buckskins, had Bill's trumpet slung around his neck. Bates had his cassette player cranked wide open, spilling "The Battle Hymn of the Republic" from its earphones, while Chester paced up and down and puffed on his cigar.

Two suspiciously nondescript sedans, both containing pairs of men in suits, were parked in front of the temple across the street. One of the men appeared to be speaking into a phone.

As soon as Traveler got out of the Jeep, Charlie hurried to the curb to clasp his hand. "Miracles require as many witnesses as possible."

Car doors opened across the street. At the same time, the Chester Building's revolving door swung into action, expelling Martin, who was carrying one of Bill's spare robes folded over his arm.

"Eleven witnesses testified to the truth of *The Book of Mormon*," Charlie said. "I count only five of us here for our testament."

"Has anyone heard from Bill?" Traveler asked.

"God will deliver him," Charlie answered.

Up the block, where Main ran into South Temple Street, a long black limousine circled Brigham Young's statue and headed their way.

"That looks like a church car to me," Martin said.

As the limousine U-turned to double-park in front of the Chester Building, Charlie began nodding as if that was exactly what he'd been expecting. But when the car door opened and Willis Tanner emerged, Charlie's nod twitched to a halt.

"This had better be good, Mo," Tanner said. "I cut short my honeymoon to be here."

"I didn't send for you," Traveler said, watching as two of the four security men crossed the road to take up positions on either side of the Chester Building's right of way. Both carried handheld radios.

"Don't look at me," Martin added.

Tanner ignored the comment to stare up at the Chester Building. "Is this place really worth all the trouble?"

"Is that why you're here?" Traveler said.

"I understand that you are a landowner on this block," Tanner said without taking his eyes from the building. "A fine temple-view lot."

"I'll deed it over to Barney if that will save his building."

"You don't know what you're dealing with, Mo."

Martin grabbed Tanner's arm. "Why don't you tell us, then? Why is Moroni's name on that deed?"

"Technically speaking, I'm not here. I'm still on my own time, honeymooning."

"That was the prophet's car you got out of."

"Do I speak for the prophet, is that what you're asking?"

"Don't you always?" Martin said. "Handling public relations is your job."

"Maybe I came here to witness Bill's return?"

"Six witnesses are better than five," Charlie said.

Martin shook his head. "Tell us about the Etinad Investment Group. Why are the Danites involved?"

"I wouldn't listen to old wives' tales if I were you," Tanner said.

"Not so fast. Do you deny that Josiah Ellsworth is more than CEO of Etinad?"

Tanner smiled.

"Do you deny that he's also the White Prophet?"

"God has only one prophet here on earth."

"Does he head the Danites or not?" Martin asked.

"The apostle Ellsworth is one of the twelve who advise the prophet."

Traveler said, "I can't help asking myself if the city would condemn land owned by an apostle without the sanction of the church."

"Success is a sign of God's love, Mo. How could we prosper if God didn't love us?"

Before Traveler could respond, Charlie raised the trumpet to his lips and sounded Bill's Cavalry Charge. Only then did Traveler see the second limousine, a silver one, turning toward them from West Temple Street. Its license plate read ETINAD.

As soon as the car stopped in front of the Chester Building, a uniformed chauffeur got out, trotted around to the rear door, and opened it. Bill emerged from the backseat carrying a seven-foot staff and one crutch. His robe, a blinding white, was unlike any Traveler had seen his friend wear before.

Bill stepped onto the sidewalk and said, "God has spoken to me. 'Seek a home, a temple for the Church of the True Prophet.' His will be done." He brought down the staff, thumping the sidewalk. "Here we will build God's temple."

Traveler glanced at Tanner to see how he was responding to the paraphrasing of Brigham Young's temple declaration spoken back in 1847. Tanner looked remarkably calm.

Bill struck the sidewalk a second time before pointing the staff at the Chester Building. "Our work is done. God's temple stands before us, ready-made. This is our tabernacle, our sanctuary. In his name, I declare it safe from secular persecution. The wrecker's ball dare not touch it."

"Bless you," Chester said.

"When Brigham's temple was completed after forty years of struggle," Bill went on, "fifty thousand people set aside their work and gathered in the streets to praise God and give the Hosanna Shout. Can we do any less?"

Nephi Bates, wide-eyed, looked from Bill to Tanner as if seeking guidance.

In unison, Bill and Charlie shouted, "Hosanna! Hosanna! Hosanna! To God and the Lamb! Amen! Amen! Amen!"

Martin said, "Good try, Bill, but I'm afraid it's too late. A church apostle has bought up most of the block."

Bill shook his head. "God has shown me the way. 'Look to the clouds,' he told me."

Traveler craned his head. There wasn't a cloud in sight, not even over the Wasatch.

"The clouds are in his temple." Bill carefully angled his staff into the revolving door before leading the way inside the Chester Building. There, standing in the center of the lobby surrounded by partially erected scaffolding, he thrust his staff into the air, pointing at the ceiling mural where Brigham Young was leading his people to their promised land. The painted sky above his wagon train was filled with billowing thunderheads, yellowed by generations of cigar smoke.

"In times past," Bill said, "I saw the face of God up there, though lately he has turned his face away from us."

"He's right," Chester said. "There used to be a face, or at least a cloud that looked like one, but I don't think it was God's."

"Whose, then?" Martin asked.

Chester shrugged. "It was already faint when I took over the building years ago."

"We must have the ceiling cleaned immediately," Bill said.

"Me and Nephi are doing the best we can," Chester said.

"Professionals are needed here."

"I can't afford to spend a fortune on a building that's going to be torn down."

Bill laid a hand on Chester's shoulder. "God will show us the way."

Traveler looked at Martin; they both knew the building's high vacancy rate had been eating away at Chester's savings for years.

Traveler said, "Go ahead and hire some help. My father and I will find the money."

"I can't do that. I—"

"It's not charity," Martin said. "We can deduct it from future rent."

"Only if there's a building." Chester blinked wetly, then waved a hand in front of his face as if to clear smoke from his eyes, despite the fact that his cigar had gone out.

Traveler turned away to test the steadiness of the scaffolding. Satisfied, he was about to climb up for a closer look at the mural when Nephi Bates announced, "The police are here."

Lieutenant Horne was leading the way through the revolving door, followed closely by his partner, Earl Belnap.

"Sanctuary!" Bill shouted as he stepped forward to bar their progress. "This is holy ground, not to be violated."

Belnap's arm snapped forward, his open palm slamming into Bill's breastbone. The Sandwich Prophet fell straight back, arms flailing, crutch and staff flying, landing flat on the granite floor hard enough to knock the wind out of him.

With a war cry, Charlie charged by Traveler, who reached for him too late. Bone cracked as the Indian's nose ran into Belnap's fist. The Indian's legs wobbled and gave out; he went down hard enough to break an elbow.

Martin lunged forward but Traveler stepped in front of him and threw a right-hand lead. In that split second before the punch landed, Belnap smiled. Then the impact hurled him onto the granite floor next to Bill.

"Hallelujah," Horne shouted. "Assault on a police officer."

Tanner shook his head at Traveler. "You ought to know better, Mo."

"I've been waiting for this a long time," Horne said, poking a finger against Traveler's chest.

"Let's not make any mistakes," Tanner said as Martin went to Charlie's aid.

"What's that supposed to mean?" Horne said.

"The way I see it, Lieutenant, a good lawyer could make a case for provocation. You know what that means. Hung juries and big fees."

Horne started to say something, snapped his teeth together instead, and helped his partner to his feet.

Once standing, Belnap grinned through a fast-swelling split lip. "I'm going to nail somebody here."

"You're damn right." Horne straightened Bill out of his fetal curl and stood him up. "This one's easy. He's already got charges pending against him."

"I'm afraid not," Tanner said.

Horne glared.

"Did you see the silver limousine outside, Lieutenant?"

Horne nodded.

"It carried Bill out of the desert," Tanner said.

Horne's face turned red; veins bulged in his neck.

Belnap grabbed Bill's wrist. "Let's cuff this bastard and be done with it."

"It's a lost cause, Earl," Horne said and escorted his sergeant outside.

Martin squinted at Tanner. "How much is this going to cost us?"

"You already owe me, Mo, for helping find your namesake."

"Tell me something, Willis," Traveler said. "Did you know all along that Moroni Traveler the Third was a girl?"

A tick started up in Tanner's left eye, a sure sign he was growing agitated. "I haven't called the debt in, have I?" He rubbed the eye. "Maybe I should, though."

"If it's the Chester Building you're thinking about," Martin said, "forget it. We've already promised Barney we'd help him."

"It's a dilemma, but I'm sure you two will see the light."

"What do you know about the deaths in Bingham?" Traveler said.

"How many favors are you asking? Debts pile up. There's interest to be paid." He stopped rubbing his eye, which remained half-closed, giving him a lopsided squint.

"Angel is all that's left of Claire," Traveler said.

"She's the only grandchild I'm ever likely to get," Martin added.

" 'Concern not yourselves about your debts,' our good book says, 'for I will give you power to pay them,' " Tanner said.

"No you don't, Willis. You've been leading Moroni astray since you were boys." Martin closed one eye, mimicking Tanner's squint. "I can quote scripture too. 'Behold, it is said in my laws, or forbidden, to get in debt to thine enemies.' "

Tanner sighed; his left eye closed altogether. "I'm telling you as a friend, your concern is not the Chester Building but Bingham. The medical report bears me out. It was murder."

THIRTY-FIVE

Traveler and Martin picked up a basket of Chicken in the Rough at the Pilot Cafe, eating dinner on the fly as they broke the speed limit all the way to Bingham. There was no traffic in the tunnel or on Main Street. Only a few houses showed lights on the hillsides. Except for the Pastime Bar and White Elephant Saloon, the business district looked deserted.

After trying the hospital, which was closed for the duration, judging by the looks of it, they tracked down Dr. Jesse Snarr at the Odegaards' house. The moment he saw them, he ushered them outside to avoid disturbing the children, who were being put to bed. The night air, maybe fifty degrees with a stiff, wind-chilling breeze, forced them back into the Jeep, with Martin and Snarr sitting up front and Traveler perched on the edge of the backseat.

Snarr spoke first. "I'm surrounded by Moronis. Unfortunately, angels, Mormon or otherwise, aren't what we need right now."

"We're here about the murder," Martin said.

"I should be surprised, since the medical report only reached me an hour ago. But the moment I met you two, I knew you weren't in Bingham for the picnic."

"We have a vested interest in this," Martin told him. "We were sitting at the same table with your parents and the Tempests. We could have been killed too."

"If I believed in such things," Snarr said, "I'd say this was the devil's work, where angels like yourself should fear to tread."

Traveler waited, expecting clarification. When none came he said, "We'd like to know what was in the report."

"It told me how it was done, and that's what makes me so goddamned mad. This is a small town, or maybe I should say *was.* Everybody knows everybody else here. Before this happened, I thought we were all friends and neighbors. Now I keep asking myself, how could any of them deliberately choose a poison like this? Think about it. Most poison tastes terrible. You couldn't disguise it if you tried. But not this one.

"It's not like you see in the movies, you know. Victims don't drink it, gasp a little, and keel over dead without much fuss. Oh, no. This one makes them suffer like a bitch bastard. It's called dimethylnitrosamine, and was developed as a solvent but soon dropped from general use because it causes liver cancer. These days it's only used to make lab animals sick."

"It sounds like you'd have to be a scientist to know about something like that," Martin said.

"Most places you would, but not in Bingham. Before they knew about the side effects, dimeth was used around here to clean mining equipment. Anybody who worked in the smelter or at the mine in recent years had access to it. If you'll switch on the car light, I'll show you what it looks like."

A moment later, Traveler saw the doctor holding a small phial of clear liquid between his forefinger and thumb.

"It looks like water, doesn't it." His voice sounded flat and emotionless, which Traveler put down to exhaustion. "A few drops in your lemonade and you get cancer, a few more and you die, just like Hannah, my parents, and Marty."

"What's the prospect for the others at the table?" Martin asked.

"So far, all their liver functions are normal."

"How much lemonade are we talking about?" Traveler said.

"Very little. Tommy said he took one sip and it wasn't sweet enough, so he tossed it away when Hattie wasn't looking. Angel says the same, but she's only three so it's hard to be sure. Garth says he drank a glass with everyone else, though he may have been confused because he was drunk."

"Will they have to be tested again?"

"We're doing that now. But the two of them didn't get so much as a stomach cramp, so my guess is they're going to be okay. What about you two? Did either of you drink the stuff?"

"No," Martin said.

Snarr slipped the phial back into his pocket and opened the door.

"Did your parents have any enemies?" Traveler asked him.

"A few days ago I would have said no."

"Did they say anything unusual before they died?"

"People that sick and in that much pain don't talk much."

The doctor stepped out of the car and stared up at the starry night. "If you're still in town tomorrow, join us at the White Elephant Saloon. Drinks are on the house and afterward we're going to bulldoze the place ourselves."

They watched Snarr walk away, then headed for the house. Martin hesitated on the narrow wooden stoop that passed for the Odegaards' front porch. "Be careful what you say if the children are still up."

Nodding, Traveler knocked softly. It was enough to bring Almon Odegaard to the door, with his wife right behind him.

"Where's Dr. Jesse gotten to?" she asked, peering around her husband.

"He said he was going for a walk," Traveler answered.

She shook her head. "I don't like him being alone at a time like this."

"I think he wanted to give us the chance to talk to you in private."

"Don't just stand there, then. Come in. Or are you trying to heat up the whole outdoors?"

In the living room, Ida settled Traveler and Martin onto the sofa, her husband into an armchair, while she took a frayed carpet-back rocker for herself.

"Has Dr. Jesse told you about the poison?" she said.

Traveler nodded.

"That boy has too big a load on his shoulders. Imagine having most of your family killed like that and suddenly find yourself with a young child to take care of."

"Now, mother, Tommy's kin. The doctor doesn't have any choice."

"Do you know what Dr. Jesse offered to do? Take care of Angel too. 'It's not right,' I told him, an unmarried man carrying so great a burden. 'Find yourself a wife,' I says, 'as soon as you can.' "

"We'd like to take care of her," Martin said.

"Mother told me we could expect something like that from you two," Odegaard said. "You've been checked on, you know. We know you're both named Moroni Traveler. So which one of you is it? Which one is Angel named after?"

"It's not up to us to ask such things," Ida interjected, rocking back and forth. "We should be happy the child has friends, though whatever happens from now on is Garth Tempest's responsibility."

"The man has to face facts, mother. That poison may kill him sometime down the line. When that happens, what happens to little Angel?"

Sighing, she picked up the pace of her rocking.

Traveler said, "Dr. Snarr told us Angel and Tommy gave up on the lemonade when they came to sit with you at the picnic."

"Thank God mother is such a good cook. If it hadn't been for her chocolate cake all three kids might be dead now."

Ida added, "They sat with us for nearly an hour, minding their manners and waiting for the cake to be cut."

She stopped rocking to retrieve a tissue from the sleeve of her dress and blow her nose. "We made a kind of a game out of it, taking turns telling stories about past picnics and cakes, things like that. If we'd only known to take Marty to the hospital then and there." She shivered and hugged herself.

"Did the children say anything unusual?" Traveler asked.

"Like what?" Odegaard said.

"Repeating something they might have heard, anything that would give us a reason for what happened."

Odegaard looked at his wife. They both shook their heads.

"Think back to the hospital, Mrs. Odegaard. Was anything said there you haven't told me about?"

"Like I said before, Hannah talked about you, Mr. Traveler. But nothing was said to explain murder."

"I was there too," Odegaard said, "visiting Lyman Snarr before he took a turn for the worse. We talked about the football game mostly. I remember him saying he was proud to have played with you, because someone had told him that you played pro ball for Los Angeles."

"That was a long time ago."

"As soon as he said it to me, I remembered seeing you on television myself. You were one hell of a linebacker, maybe the best ever to come out of this state. When I said so to Garth later on he got mad as hell. He said you had no business playing if you were a professional, that you could have hurt somebody. If you asked me, he was just feeling foolish, because he tried to take you on during the game. It wasn't your idea to play, I told him. I was the one who insisted. I'm glad you played with us, though. Beating the crap out of those company men, especially Father Bannon and Frank Murdock, did my heart good."

"Now, father," Ida said, "calm down. You don't want to be up all night with indigestion."

He grunted. "First thing tomorrow morning I'm meeting that man from the Historical Society—Mr. Pinock—and we're going to take one last walk through town. He's going to tape-record my comments as the last mayor of Bingham Canyon."

"I'd like to be there to hear you," Martin said.

"You're welcome to join us."

"There's only one way they can do that, father. We'll have to put them both up on the screen porch."

THIRTY-SIX

While Martin toured the town with Mayor Odegaard and Wayne Pinock the next morning, Traveler followed Ida's directions to Frank Murdock's house, an unpainted wooden shack like all the others backing up against the steep hillside behind Carr Fork. The only sign of life on the street was a new blue Mercedes-Benz, which Ida had told Traveler to watch for. The car's trunk stood open, as did the shack's front door.

Traveler knocked on the clapboard to announce himself to the square, heavyset man who was inside on his knees, rolling up a small threadbare rug. He twitched at the sound and swung around, squinting against the light.

"It's me, Mr. Murdock, Moroni Traveler."

"Sure, from the football game. I remember." He lumbered to his feet. "Come on in. I was just taking inventory."

The small front room was bare of everything but a battered chest of drawers, a small-screen TV with rabbit ears, and the half-rolled rug that was worn to the backing in places.

"You kicked our asses but good in that game," Murdock said. "You made us look like a bunch of amateurs."

"I shouldn't have played."

"Are you kidding? We'll all be telling that story for years to come, cadging free drinks by lying about how we knocked Moroni Traveler on his ass. When you think of it that way, you did us a favor."

"Maybe you can do me one in return?"

"Try me."

"I'm here about the murders," Traveler said.

"Jesus Christ! Are you telling me it wasn't an accident?"

Traveler handed him a business card.

"That does it. Maybe my timing's lousy, but I can't help saying good riddance to this place."

Traveler said nothing, hoping to keep Murdock talking.

"Look around you," Murdock said to end the silence. "My parents lived in this dump all their lives. I thought the same thing was going to happen to me until Kennecott offered to buy me out. Well, God bless them, that's what I say."

"I was sitting with the Snarrs and the Tempests at the picnic," Traveler said. "I'm alive and here talking to you because I didn't drink the lemonade."

Murdock squinted at him. "After playing against you, I wouldn't want you mad at me, that's for sure. But you've come to the wrong man for answers. I don't know a damned thing, except maybe a little local gossip. But nothing about the Snarrs or the Tempests that would cause a murder."

"They tell me you're one of the biggest landowners here."

Murdock snorted. "That's people for you, talking behind your back. Sure, I inherited half a dozen places from my father. All like this one, with nobody willing to rent them anymore. If Kennecott hadn't wanted to take them off my hands, they wouldn't be good for anything but kindling."

He opened the chest's top drawer and took out a silver-framed wedding photograph that had turned sepia around the edges. "These are my parents, Isaac and Melba. They worked all their lives in Bingham. They never took vacations, never spent a dime extra on themselves. Dad drove a Hudson, the only car I ever remember him having, till the day he died. I asked him once why he'd didn't buy something better, and those were the days when you could still rent these places and he had some income. Do you know what he said? 'You don't give up on something that's served you well, just because it's getting old.' Well, that's not for me. Did you see that kraut car parked outside? I bought it the day Kennecott put its offer in writing."

He handed the photograph to Traveler. It looked old-fashioned enough to be a pioneer daguerreotype, though the Murdocks' wedding couldn't have been much more than forty years ago, judging by their son's age.

"You can't tell it from looking at him," Murdock said, "but my father had miner's hands, like sandpaper they were. The grime works its way in under your skin, and you can't get it out no matter what you do. Try running those over a pretty woman's skin and see how far it gets you."

He paused to examine his own callused fingers. "You know where I'm going from here? To Salt Lake. I'm getting myself a condo in one of those big downtown buildings and live like a king. Once a week I'm going to find myself a fancy barber-shop and have myself a manicure."

Kennecott's warning siren went off, just over the mountain by the sound of it. Traveler handed back the photograph, which Murdock quickly stowed between two lace tablecloths in the chest. The blast came, shaking the house, before he got the drawer closed.

"You know what my mother called this chest?" Murdock said, still holding on to the piece of furniture. "Her hope chest. 'Monkey Ward's best,' she used to tell me. 'Your father and I bought it the day we were married, to store our treasures.' There's a family Bible in here somewhere with a pressed rose from her wedding bouquet between the pages. That, the table-cloths and shawls she crocheted, plus a few keepsakes and my old report cards are all the treasures she ever got."

He kicked the bottom drawer. "A *no hope* chest, that's what I call it. I ought to throw the damned thing out along with everything else."

Murdock shook his head violently. "I know what they're saying about me. That's why you're here, to see just what kind of a company man I am. Well, all I can say is this. I never want to see this town or another mine in my life. If it wasn't that I wanted to say good-bye to a few friends, I'd leave right now and take a pass on the farewell party down at the White Elephant tonight."

"Maybe I'll see you there," Traveler said.

"You watch yourself once those miners and smelter men start drinking. A little Dutch courage and they'll be taking shots at you like we did in the game."

"Did you know who I was then?"

"Not at first, but someone in the huddle recognized you."

"Who?"

"I can't remember. Some of the guys were good and pissed, though. A pro shouldn't take sides, they said. That's why they . . . why a few of them took shots at you, I guess."

"I got clipped a couple of times."

"I remember. It was Father Bannon. He came back to the huddle and said, 'Watch out. I think I got him mad that time.' " Murdock caught his breath. "Oh, Christ. Is that why you and Garth Tempest got into it?"

Traveler remembered Tempest coming at him like a maniac late in the game.

"It didn't strike me then," Murdock said, "that his daughter was named Moroni Traveler Tempest. He had a grudge against you, didn't he?"

Traveler shrugged. "Is Father Bannon still in town?"

"He was at his church when I drove by a few minutes ago."

Traveler thanked Murdock and left the house, heading downhill toward the Holy Rosary Catholic Church on Main Street. At the fork in the road, he looked back to see Murdock loading his mother's "hope chest" into the backseat of his new Mercedes-Benz.

THIRTY-SEVEN

A flatbed truck carrying a bulldozer chained to its back was parked in front of the Holy Rosary Church. The driver, a darkly tanned man wearing a bright yellow hard hat, stood in front of the church's open door gesturing to someone inside. By the time Traveler joined the driver, a second workman, also in hard hat, emerged from the clapboard church accompanied by Father Bannon.

"Take a last look, Mr. Traveler," Bannon said. "There won't be anything left of this place by dark." He looked at the driver, who nodded agreement to that statement. "There's not much to these old places, they tell me. They come down like a house of cards. You'd think a house of worship would be more substantial."

The driver and his cohort exchanged looks and fled toward the flatbed as if fearing a sermon.

"I thought I'd be glad to be rid of this place. Now . . ." The priest nudged Traveler onto the threshold to point out a stained-glass Madonna and child glowing in the morning light behind the altar.

Traveler was about to walk down the center aisle when Joe Balic, the Orthodox priest, parked his car behind the truck, stepped out into the middle of Main Street, put both hands to the small of his back, and stared up at the church's two-story wooden spire.

"I'd offer you a seat, old man," Bannon called out good-naturedly, "but the pews are gone, sold off and hauled away by some antique dealer."

Shaking his head, Balic joined them at the front door.

"We got no takers for the stained glass," Bannon said. "It's too badly cracked because of the blasting."

Balic dismissed the comment with a backhanded wave. "It's the memories that count, the history. Think about it, Father. Generations have gathered here for services. God alone knows what confessions were heard here over the years, especially back in the days when Bingham's red-light district was going full blast. I know. I grew old up here in this canyon."

Bannon raised an eyebrow. "And I'm a newcomer, is that what you're saying?"

The old priest smiled. "I envy you the long road ahead."

"I don't know how far I'll get with the load I'm carrying. I wanted a parish in Salt Lake, a large congregation, not the handful I was ministering to here. And why? For pride's sake, I realize now, not for God's. I wanted an audience. I wanted success. To get it, I took sides. I wanted the town sold. Now people are dead because of the enmity I helped arouse."

He looked at Traveler. "You have every right to accuse me," Bannon said. "Even at the football game, I caused trouble. For all I know, the fire I lit there turned to hatred and murder."

"I don't understand," Balic said.

"Mr. Traveler does, I think. Do you remember when we first started playing? Traveler wasn't really trying all that hard. That's when I took a couple of cheap shots at him because he was on the other side, the side that wanted to fight the company buyout. I told the others, too. 'Take a shot at the old pro,' I said. I thought it was funny at the time, since you didn't seem to want to fight back."

"*You* told them who I was?" Traveler said.

"Sure. During one of the huddles, or maybe it was a beer timeout. 'That's Moroni Traveler,' I said. "He used to play linebacker for L.A.' You'd been calling yourself Martin."

"What did Garth Tempest say?"

"Something I won't repeat."

"Did you know his daughter's full name?" Traveler asked.

Bannon shook his head.

"Her name's Moroni Traveler Tempest," Balic supplied. "Angel for short."

"Dear God," Bannon said.

Traveler touched the bruise on his forehead where Tempest had hit him during the game.

"I'm an old man," Balic said. "I don't want to pass on with a child on my conscience."

"I agree," Bannon said.

The two priests stared at each other for a moment. Finally, the younger man nodded, giving way to Father Balic. "There are people in this town, people I trust, who say Garth Tempest beat his wife. I never saw it happen myself, and Hannah never said a word to me. She wasn't my parishioner, though I did see her looking the worse for wear on a number of occasions."

"She attended my church," Bannon said.

"We can't ask you to break the seal of the confessional," Balic told him.

"Is it true?" Traveler asked. "Did he abuse her?"

Bannon turned away, but not before Traveler saw the answer on his face.

Traveler clenched his teeth. "And the child?"

The priest walked away without answering.

THIRTY-EIGHT

Traveler went looking for Garth Tempest but found Martin and Wayne Pinock first, drinking a lunchtime beer at the White Elephant Saloon along with half a dozen others, none of whom he knew by sight. Hand-lettered signs taped to the mirror behind the bar said, OFFICIAL FAREWELL PARTY STARTS AT 6. EVERYTHING MUST GO, DRINKABLE OR NOT. Crepe-paper streamers had been draped through the dozen or so deer antlers that decorated the walls.

Martin took one look at Traveler and said, "You look like you're about to explode."

Traveler shook his head and ordered a beer. He didn't speak until it was gone. "I've just come from the Tempest place, but no one was home."

"We ran into Garth Tempest half an hour ago," Pinock said. "Up at his souvenir shop."

"There's no hurry to catch him," Martin added, his eyes never leaving Traveler's face. "He told us he'd be at the Copper Keepsake most of the day, packing up for the movers."

"Before you go looking for him," Pinock said, "your father

and I have got news. Not five minutes ago we got off the phone to the Chester Building. Your friend Bill was right about the mural. They've been cleaning the ceiling all day and there is a face in the clouds."

"Barney says it looks a little like Joseph Smith," Martin said. "Joe's spirit, anyway, looking down from heaven to oversee his flock's trek to the promised land. Barney's words anyway, or maybe Bill's. The bunch of them sounded like they'd been celebrating."

"We're going to meet there first thing tomorrow," Pinock added, "so I can photograph their discovery. If Thomas Hart Benton painted Joseph Smith, the Historical Society will want it fully documented. So far as I can remember, the Gustavson collection showed no close-ups of the clouds. I copied a few prints, though, and I'll bring them along for comparison."

"We'll be there," Traveler said. "Now, if you'll excuse us."

Without a word, Martin followed him outside. "Jesus Christ, Moroni. You should see the look on your face. What the hell's going on?"

"Garth Tempest knew who I was during the football game. Father Bannon told him."

"No wonder he tried to take your head off."

"The priest says he beat Hannah."

"And Angel?" Martin asked.

"I don't know, but I want you covering my back when I talk to him."

"Don't I always?"

THIRTY-NINE

Kennecott's warning siren sounded as Traveler opened the door to the Copper Keepsake. The shop, already a shambles, shook violently when the blast came a moment later. A string of shiny cowbells, hanging like a mobile from the low-raftered ceiling, clanged loudly. The few copper souvenirs left on the shelves began tumbling onto the floor where Garth Tempest stood, surrounded by partially filled packing boxes. The shaking raised enough dust to make Traveler's eyes water.

"For Christ's sake!" Tempest shouted. "You'd think they could let us leave in peace."

Behind the waist-high customer counter a child began to whimper. When Traveler edged past Tempest to peer over the barrier, he saw Angel's tear-streaked, dirty face. She grew quiet at the sight of him and stuck a thumb in her mouth.

"I thought she was staying with the Odegaards," Traveler said.

"I'll tell you the same thing I told them. Keep your nose out of my business." Tempest moved behind the counter to stand beside Angel.

"I'm a detective," Traveler said.

"I know all about you. When the police talked to me, I gave them your name. 'Talk to him,' I said. 'He seems to know more about my life than I do. He's responsible. Nobody died until he showed up.' "

"The poison was a solvent used to clean mining equipment."

"I've never met anyone named for an angel before," Tempest said. "Except *my* daughter."

Traveler glanced over his shoulder to reassure himself that Martin was standing outside the shop window.

"If you had any balls," Tempest said, "you'd tell me the truth."

"About what?"

Tempest looked down at the girl, who was wearing shorts and a T-shirt. "I know my slut wife named her after you. Miss Moroni Traveler Tempest." He clenched his teeth so hard veins stood out in his neck. "What a laugh you must have had about that, fucking my wife and sticking me with your kid."

"I never met your wife before I came here."

"Sure. Tell me another one. Mr. Sucker who believes his wife after she walks out on him, stays away nine months, and then comes back with his baby."

"The child's real mother was Claire Bennion. She named Angel after me. Your wife had to promise to keep the name before Claire would agree to an adoption."

Tempest twitched. " 'Look,' Hannah says to me when she hands me the kid, 'she has your eyes, your coloring.' And me buying it, too dumb to know she'd been spreading her legs for someone like you. How was she, huh? Did she—"

Traveler leaned over the counter, grabbed Tempest's shirt, and shook him. "Keep your mouth shut in front of your daughter."

"You should be dead, goddamn you. A man named for an angel shouldn't drink beer. I thought you were a Mormon. Mormons drink lemonade."

Traveler threw the punch without thinking. Even as it landed, he saw the terror on Angel's face. The impact of the blow hurled Tempest into the wall shelves behind him, which broke free of their brackets. Traveler lunged headfirst across the counter, using his own body to shield Angel from the falling debris. He was about to pick her up when Tempest's fist caught him on the back of the neck, slamming his chin against the countertop and sinking his teeth into his tongue.

Despite the pain, he left himself vulnerable and continued to shield her. But Tempest didn't follow up. When Traveler turned his head to see why, Martin was standing in the open doorway, holding a .45.

Carefully, Traveler cleared away the debris. As soon as he freed Angel, she ran to her father and wrapped her arms around his legs, sobbing.

"To think I invited you to share my food," Tempest said.

At a nod from Traveler, Martin handed over the .45 before retreating outside, where he kept watch from the curb across the street.

Tempest glared at the top of his daughter's head. "God was on my side at that football game. I knew that when Father Bannon called me over. 'You see that big bastard,' he said, 'that's Moroni Traveler. He used to play in the pros.' After that all I could think about was your name. Moroni fucking Traveler. 'We'll name her Moroni, after the angel,' Hannah told me. I wanted to kill you then and there. I tried to kill you, but it was no use. I wasn't big enough. That's when I got the idea. I had the solvent in my trunk. I shouldn't have had it, you know. It's too dangerous. They told us that at the mine, that it caused cancer. Only I'd seen how well it cleaned the machinery, so I figured it would do the same for my car engine. I told myself it would be all right as long as I was careful. Only I never got around to using it."

"But you drank some of that lemonade yourself," Traveler said.

"I took a handful of aspirin to make myself sick."

"What about Angel and Tommy?"

"There was no need. By the time the kids left for the chocolate cake, the guilty had already done their drinking, so I pretended to find a bug in the lemonade and dumped it out."

"And Marty?"

"Once he drank it, there was nothing I could do."

The .45 shook in Traveler's hand. "If it was me you were after, why kill the Snarrs?"

"Hannah stayed with them those nine months. They had to know the child wasn't mine. They lied for her, they covered up her adultery."

Traveler looked at Angel, who continued to hide her face against Tempest's leg.

"Believe me," Traveler said, "it wasn't your wife who was unfaithful. She wanted a child and Claire Bennion came along. That's all there is to it."

Tempest shook his leg. "Let go, Angel."

She didn't budge.

"You were the only one who was supposed to die," Tempest said. "I wanted to give the rest of them cancer. I wanted them to suffer a long time. I wanted them to pay for what they'd done to me."

He grabbed hold of Angel's ear and twisted it until she cried out. "You let go of me when I tell you." He kicked out suddenly, throwing her against the counter and knocking the wind out of her. Her shorts rode up far enough to expose old bruises on her thighs.

Traveler released the safety and raised the pistol. Out of the corner of his eye he saw Martin running toward the shop.

"You can't shoot me." Tempest smiled. "You have no proof, and a three-year-old bastard child can't testify."

Martin opened the door.

Without another word, Tempest walked out into the street. Traveler followed onto the sidewalk where he took careful aim at the man's retreating back.

Martin touched Traveler on the shoulder. "My grandchild's watching you."

Traveler watched Tempest out of sight before handing the .45 back to Martin.

"What happened?" Martin said.

Quietly, Traveler summarized Tempest's confession. As soon as he finished speaking, Martin said, "I'll take her to the Odegaards for safekeeping."

Nodding, Traveler headed for the White Elephant Saloon where Garth Tempest had disappeared.

FORTY

The only cars on Main Street were parked in front of the saloon. Inside, a crowd of maybe twenty people was getting a midafternoon start on the evening's farewell party. Most looked to be old-timers, men still lean enough to wear jeans low on their hips, but with stomachs that overlapped their belt buckles. At a guess, Traveler placed smelter men at one end of the bar, miners at the other, with a knot of pale shopkeepers, Garth Tempest among them, in the center. As promised, Dr. Jesse Snarr was behind the bar where half a dozen whiskey bottles, at various levels of depletion, stood at regular intervals.

Traveler took a quick breath of fresh air and plunged across the threshold into the thick cloud of cigarette and cigar smoke. The conversation lulled as the men turned away from the bar to stare at him.

"Just the man," someone said from among the smelter group. As one, they waved him over; the miners came too, even the shopkeepers, though Tempest held back.

"The name's Zeke," the man who'd spoken said, shaking hands. "We've been talking about that football game at the picnic." He looked around, received nods of encouragement from his cronies, and continued. "I say a professional linebacker's just like a boxer. If he hits someone it's as good as using a gun."

"I was holding back at the picnic," Traveler said.

"Jesus," Zeke said. "I'd hate to see you playing for real."

Another man said, "I saw you play for L.A. You crippled some running back, I remember that. Put the gazooney in a wheelchair for life."

Traveler, feigning nonchalance, glared at Tempest. "In the pros, you had to hurt people to keep up your reputation."

"We could have used you during the strike," Zeke said.

"That was before my time."

"Hell. That was before everyone's time." Zeke's comment produced laughter from his cohorts. As soon as it subsided, another man said, "Our fathers told us what it was like, though. Company spies and gunmen were everywhere, doing their best to intimidate us workers. They killed Joe Hill, the union man, that's for sure."

"Give the man a break!" Snarr shouted from behind the bar. "He looks like he could use a drink."

The men parted to let Traveler through to the bar, where Snarr immediately filled a shot glass with whiskey and drew a mug of beer from the tap.

"Don't mind them." The hollows under the doctor's eyes were smudged with exhaustion. "They're reliving the past to keep from thinking about the future, when their town's gone for good."

Traveler gulped his whiskey while watching Tempest's reflection in the bar mirror.

"I know how you feel," Snarr said. "I tried to get drunk myself last night but ended up sick instead."

"More beer," someone shouted.

"My patients need me." Snarr moved down the bar refilling mugs.

Tempest now stood at the far end of the bar, near the White Elephant's back door. Except for Traveler, everyone else had gathered at the front of the saloon.

Traveler pointed a finger at Tempest's reflection and fired an imaginary round. The man turned toward the rear door in time to see it opened by Martin.

From the front of the saloon came the cry, "Let's hear it for Joe Hill!"

The song started raggedly but quickly grew in volume.

> "I dreamed I saw Joe Hill last night
>> Alive as you and me.
> Says I, 'But Joe, you're ten years dead.'
>> 'I never died,' says he.
>> 'I never died,' says he.
>
> 'In Salt Lake, Joe, by God,' says I,
>> Him standing by my bed,
> 'They framed you on a murder charge.'
>> Says Joe, 'I didn't die.'
>> Says Joe, 'I didn't die.' "

Traveler hadn't remembered the words, but he did know the story. Joe Hill, an organizer for the old IWW, the Industrial Workers of the World known as Wobblies, had been convicted and executed about the time of the First World War at the instigation of the Utah Copper Company, the forerunner of Kennecott. Or so the union litany went.

> " 'For the copper bosses, they framed you, Joe.'
>> 'They shot you, Joe,' says I.
> 'Takes more than guns to kill a man.'
>> Says Joe, 'I did not die.'
>> Says Joe, 'I did not die.' "

Traveler walked down the bar until he was close enough to Garth Tempest to be heard over the singing. "If I remember my history," Traveler said, "they tied Joe to a kitchen chair and shot him at the old Sugar House prison." He looked around as if seeking a similar chair.

"These are my friends in here," Tempest said. "They'll protect me."

"For how long?"

"You're not going to catch me outside alone, if that's what you're getting at. I'll stay here all night if I have to."

Before Traveler could respond, Snarr came down the bar to refill their glasses. When he saw Martin standing at the back door, he waved him over and poured another drink.

Rather than be sandwiched between Traveler and Martin, Tempest fled toward the front of the saloon, where the others were beginning another stanza.

"And standing there as big as life
And smiling with his eyes,
Joe says, 'What they forgot to kill
Went on to organize,
Went on to organize.'

'Joe Hill ain't dead,' he says to me,
'Joe Hill ain't never died.
Where working men are out on strike
Joe Hill is at their side.
Joe Hill is at their side.' "

When the singing stopped, Martin looked at Traveler. "You'd better tell Dr. Snarr what happened."

Traveler decided to get it over with as quickly as possible. "Garth Tempest poisoned the lemonade. He told me so himself."

"What's the joke? Why would he do something like that?" Snarr said.

"Angel wasn't his daughter. She was named for me. I was the one he wanted dead. He mistook me for a Mormon because of my name and thought I'd drink lemonade instead of beer."

When Snarr shook his head in disbelief, Martin quickly summarized Traveler's relationship with Claire.

"Hold it," Snarr said finally. "Garth drank some of that

lemonade too. He was sick as a dog. I saw him throwing up myself."

"He told me he took a handful of aspirin," Traveler said.

"Son of a bitch. That would explain the tests, why his liver functions are perfectly normal." Snarr drank directly from the whiskey bottle he was holding. When he came up for air he said, "But that doesn't explain why he would kill my parents, or my brother either, for that matter."

"He blamed them for keeping the truth about Angel from him. He didn't want them to die quickly, he told me. He wanted them to suffer first. As for your little brother, Tempest says that was an accident."

The half-empty bottle trembled in Snarr's hand. "The bastard! Why did he have to use something like dimeth? Have you ever seen anyone die of liver cancer?"

Traveler shook his head.

"I have, goddammit." With his free hand, the doctor rubbed his face as if trying to remove the pain reflected there. "You and your father get out of here. Now!"

Traveler looked at Martin, who shrugged and left the way he'd come.

"I can go to the police with you," Traveler said.

Snarr glared.

"You have Tommy to think about."

"Good-bye, Mr. Traveler."

Traveler looked for Tempest who, though surrounded by miners and smelter men, was staring back, looking smug.

Snarr turned his back on the crowd. Visible in the mirror, but only from Traveler's angle, Snarr removed a phial from his pocket and poured some of the liquid into the whiskey bottle he was holding.

A few drops and you get cancer, Traveler remembered as he walked toward the door. *A few more and you die.*

"Come on, Garth," Snarr shouted, "it's time to drink to the loved ones we've lost."

FORTY-ONE

At seven the next morning Traveler and Martin expected to have the Chester Building to themselves. But Bill and Charlie were there ahead of them, as was Barney Chester, Nephi Bates, and Wayne Pinock from the Historical Society. Pinock had already set up half a dozen camera lights around the base of the metal scaffolding and was now focusing their beams on the freshly cleaned ceiling mural. Several NO SMOKING signs, done in Chester's hand, had been taped to the scaffolding's crossbeams.

"There's definitely a face in those clouds," Pinock announced once he'd adjusted the last of his lights. He looked at Chester. "Did you find a signature during the cleaning?"

Chester shook his head. "We didn't have your lights to work with."

"I'd better climb up there and take a look for myself, then, hadn't I?"

An aluminum stepladder got Pinock started. After that, he used the scaffolding's metal beams for footholds. His weight caused the entire structure to wobble precariously.

Traveler grabbed hold to stabilize it; the others joined him.

"Better him than me," Martin muttered, staring up at the ceiling thirty feet above.

Once on top, Pinock began examining the mural with a magnifying glass, concentrating on the thunderheads looming above Brigham Young's wagon train. He went back and forth across a ten-foot section twice before nodding to himself.

"The likeness is definitely Joseph Smith," he shouted down. "The style looks familiar too, but I don't think it's Thomas Hart Benton."

"I told you before, " Bill said. "God's up there."

"Joseph Smith isn't God," Chester said, winking to show that he knew Mormons who thought otherwise.

"The WPA photos are in my case," Pinock called out. "Will someone bring them to me?"

Traveler looked around for volunteers. Bill and Charlie folded their arms and sat cross-legged, like Indians. Bates retreated to his elevator while Chester fussed with an unlit cigar.

Martin said, "A man my age shouldn't exert himself."

Groaning, Traveler fetched the photos and climbed up top with Pinock, who sorted through the shots until he found one that showed two artists standing on a similar scaffolding more than fifty years ago. The WPA mural behind them was in focus, but not their faces.

"I snitched this one from the Gustavson collection before Gussie took it back."

"I wouldn't know Thomas Hart Benton if I saw him." Traveler's voice echoed off the ceiling.

"The one on the left could be him."

"Why don't you ask me?" Bill shouted.

Traveler leaned over the edge. "You haven't seen it close up yet."

"I saw it in my revelation."

"I'm listening."

"Look to *The Book of Mormon.*"

That didn't sound like Bill, who claimed to be writing his own holy book for what he and Charlie called their Church of the True Prophet.

"Us prophets must stick together," Bill clarified.

"We don't have time to go through more than a thousand pages," Traveler said.

"The name is Mahonri," Bill answered. "I can say no more."

Pinock snapped his fingers. "He's right. I recognized the style now. It looks like Mahonri Young."

Traveler peered over the side again to see Charlie and Bill slap hands and then immediately begin loading a long-stemmed pipe from the Indian's full peyote bag.

"He drew me to the Sea Gull Monument," Bill announced.

"Who?" Traveler asked.

"The White Prophet, or maybe Mahonri himself."

"If he's right and this is Mahonri's work," Pinock said, "it could be a godsend."

Mahonri Young, the last of Brigham Young's grandchildren to be born during the prophet's lifetime, was Utah's most famous artist. The Sea Gull Monument was his creation, as was the monument at the mouth of Emigration Canyon that marked the spot where Brigham Young first set eyes on the Great Salt Lake Valley and told the members of his wagon train that they were home at last.

"We're going to need proof," Pinock said.

Together, he and Traveler went over every inch of Joseph Smith's face. They were about to extend their search to the surrounding thunderheads when Pinock found a signature, *Mahonri*, hidden in the prophet's hairline.

"I'll take some close-ups of this," Pinock said. "If that doesn't do the trick, we'll get an art expert in here to verify the signature. While I'm at it, I'll have blowups made of the artist's face in that old photo. With luck, computer enhancement will put Mahonri into focus."

"Do you need anything from me?"

When Pinock said no, Traveler launched himself over the side and scrambled down the scaffolding. At floor level he stood eye-to-eye with Bill. "Talk to me about Josiah Ellsworth."

"I thought Charlie told you. He appeared to me in the desert."

"You said God appeared."

Bill lit his pipe and took a long drag, holding the smoke in as long as possible. When it began leaking from his mouth, Chester pulled a NO SMOKING sign from the scaffolding and waved it in Bill's face.

"Religious freedom's at stake," Charlie said, patting that medicine bag hanging from his neck.

Chester pointed at the ceiling. "You and Bill will clean it yourselves next time Joe Smith disappears."

"I didn't mean to say God came to us in the desert," Bill said. "He sent a representative." He sucked on the pipe until his face took on a dreamy expression. "Follow me." Using one crutch, he moved across the lobby to the front window—with Traveler, Martin, Barney Chester, and Charlie right behind him—and tapped on the glass. "He was there, on the temple grounds, when I climbed among the seagulls."

"Spit it out, Bill," Traveler said. "Are you talking about Josiah Ellsworth or not?"

" 'Tell Moroni I do this for him,' the White Prophet told me in the desert."

"Which Moroni?" Martin asked.

"Dammit," Traveler said. "White Prophet or not, the man also put my name on a deed. Will someone tell me if I'm related to him or not?"

Martin sighed. "My contact at the City and County Building now says your name's been removed from the deed. It was all a mistake, I'm told. A clerical error."

Bill nodded dreamily. "He told me, 'Moroni must be taken care of one way or another.' "

Traveler glared at Martin, who shrugged. "Your mother was always a mystery to me."

"Will someone come back here and hold the ladder for me?" Pinock shouted. "If I get to the lab right away, we ought to have our answer by noon."

FORTY-TWO

Willis Tanner entered the Chester Building at noon precisely; he had Wayne Pinock in tow. By then the lobby had been turned into an Indian campground, with two sets of tepeed sandwich boards providing sleeping shelters for Bill and Charlie, who claimed exhaustion after their desert ordeal, though Traveler suspected that an excess of religious, peyote-induced zeal explained their comatose state.

Tanner joined Traveler and Martin at the cigar stand, where they were drinking coffee with Barney Chester. A fresh NO SMOKING sign had been taped to the front of the display case near the eternal flame, now repaired and burning without so much as a flicker.

"If you'll excuse us, Barney," Tanner said, "I'd like to talk to my Moronis alone for a moment." Tanner walked into the men's room without waiting for a reply.

As soon as Traveler and Martin joined him there, Tanner began checking the stalls. Once certain they were empty he said, "Garth Tempest has been hospitalized."

"How bad?" Traveler asked.

"They're calling it a relapse. They say his system must have been full of poison all along. That he must have been more resistant than the others."

"What does Tempest say?" Traveler said.

"Nothing. He slipped into a coma just like the others and isn't expected to live."

Martin said, "You could have told us this in front of Barney. So what are you holding back?"

"I thought you'd want privacy when you learned that Moroni Traveler Tempest is about to become an orphan."

"Where is she?" Martin asked.

"She'll be staying with the Odegaards until the legal system gears up to place her in a foster home."

Martin sighed.

"What about the Chester Building?" Traveler said.

"Barney ought to be in on this."

As soon as they returned to the lobby, Pinock began switching on his floodlights. Once the ceiling was illuminated, Tanner slowly circled the scaffolding, his head thrust back as he studied the mural. Finally, he signaled to Pinock, who extinguished the lights.

"If you don't mind, Barney," Tanner said when he returned to the cigar stand, "we'd like to leave the scaffold and lights in place for a while. That way scholars will have a chance to come and see this for themselves. Put their stamp of approval on it, so to speak."

Chester shrugged. "What do I have to lose?" He poured a cup of coffee for Tanner.

"Is that Postum?"

"Of course," Chester said, though everyone knew it was a lie.

Sipping, Tanner made a wry face.

"I know that look of yours," Traveler said. "You already know the verdict on the ceiling."

At a nod from Tanner, Pinock retrieved a folder from his briefcase and hurried forward to spread photographs on top of the cigar counter. They were blowups of the two WPA painters from the Gustavson collection. Their enlarged faces were much sharper than the original photographs. One face was circled in fluorescent Day-Glo orange.

"It's Mahonri Young, all right," Tanner said. "We've verified it."

"What does that mean exactly?" Chester said.

"Your ceiling's a treasure, Barney. No doubt about it. Word of your discovery has already been passed on to the prophet."

"Which one?" Traveler said.

Tanner ignored the question. "He asked me to thank all of you for saving an important part of our heritage. We fully expect the faithful to be making pilgrimages here soon to see your ceiling."

"Are you saying my building's safe?"

"It's a shrine, Barney, the first prophet painted by the grandson of our second prophet. It's already been added to the register of historic sites."

Chester's lips moved but no words came out. In frustration, he threw his arms around Tanner, who squirmed awkwardly.

As soon as the clinch broke, Traveler glared at Tanner. "Talk to me, Willis. Somebody pointed Bill and Charlie in the right direction. They say it was the White Prophet."

Tanner tapped his toe against Bill's sandaled feet protruding from the sandwich-board tepee. "Who am I to question another man's revelation?"

"Why would Ellsworth help us?"

Tanner stared at the ceiling. "A vision of Joseph Smith was saved. As a result, all charges have been dropped against Bill and Charlie. The prophet has seen to that. Obviously, their trespass on the temple grounds was part of God's plan."

Traveler grabbed Tanner's arm. "You're the expert, Willis. Am I related to Ellsworth?"

"We must know our ancestors, Mo, both living and dead. That is the commandment that God gave to Joseph Smith."

"You sound as vague as Martin."

Tanner smiled. " 'Tell my Moronis,' the prophet said to me before I came here, 'that I honor them for their work. Without their efforts, one of God's treasures would have been lost. We are in your debt.' His words, Mo. I repeat them as spoken. 'If there's anything I can do for my Moronis, all they have to do is ask.' "

"Now that you mention it," Martin said, "there is some legal paperwork we could use a hand with. The adoption of my granddaughter."

"Actually, that's already in the works. In this state, the courts listen carefully when the prophet speaks, and he has decided that Lael and I should adopt Angel. 'Naturally,' the prophet said, 'my other two Moronis will have full visiting privileges. Moronis, no matter who they're named for,' he said, 'cannot be separated.' "

"Glory hallelujah," Bill shouted from inside his sandwich-board teepee.

"We can do better than that," Martin said. "Come on, Mo, hold the ladder for me."

As soon as Martin reached the top of the scaffolding, he led them in the Hosanna Shout.